Neil's gentle words touched her heart

"When I first saw you standing in my doorway in the twilight with your hair hanging like a wimple around your face, I thought for a moment you were the ghost of some Highland lady come to haunt this place," Neil murmured.

"And when I saw you with your rod, I thought you were a clan chieftain with your sword, come to claim me as your lady," Kirsty whispered back.

"It seems we share similar fantasies," he replied. As a strange indefinable longing to share more with him swept over her, Kristy placed her hands on his shoulders as he knelt before her and bent her head to his so that their lips touched in a kiss.

FLORA KIDD
is also the author of these

Harlequin Presents

and these
Harlequin Romances

Many of these books are available at your local bookseller.

For a free catalog listing all titles currently available,
send your name and address to:

HARLEQUIN READER SERVICE
1440 South Priest Drive, Tempe, AZ 85281
Canadian address: Stratford, Ontario N5A 6W2

FLORA KIDD

tempted to love

Harlequin Books

TORONTO • NEW YORK • LOS ANGELES • LONDON
AMSTERDAM • PARIS • SYDNEY • HAMBURG
STOCKHOLM • ATHENS • TOKYO • MILAN

Harlequin Presents first edition March 1983
ISBN 0-373-10577-0

Original hardcover edition published in 1982
by Mills & Boon Limited

CHAPTER ONE

UNDER the hot July sky, flecked here and there with tiny white clouds, the silvery waters of Loch Lannach were dulled by a shimmering heat haze. High up on the slope of Autnoch Hill four people walked, a woman and three men.

The men all walked ahead of the woman, in single file as they followed a steep path which dropped from the slope into a wooded glen made by the Lannach River, a narrow sparkling stream, babbling serenely over smooth ledges of basalt rock between cliffs of reddish sandstone.

When she reached the path winding beside the river the woman slowed down. Tall and slender, she was dressed in pants made from a red and green tartan, the MacGregor tartan, which she was entitled to wear because her married surname was Whyte, and the Whytes are a sept of the MacGregor clan. Her blouse was a soft shade of green and she wore an oatmeal-coloured hand-knitted sweater tied casually by its sleeves around her neck. On her feet were wellington boots, the best sort of footwear for the countryside of the Scottish Highlands.

She walked with easy strides beside the stream. Thin shafts of sunlight slanting between the leaves of the birches willows and hazels crowding along the river banks glinted on her thick black

hair, which she wore coiled into a knot on top of
her head. Wisps of hair escaped from the knot to
twist delicately and intriguingly about her lightly
sun-tanned heart-shaped face. Beneath fine arching eyebrows her eyes were a brilliant blue, their
expression one of smiling pleasure as she looked
at the trees. Once or twice she reached out a hand
to smooth the silvery bark of a birch as if she
were greeting an old friend.

The higher she walked after the men the less the
stream became, until half its bed was dry and water
was no more than a series of pools linked together
by beds of wet shingle scattered with reddish
rocks. On either side the cliffs rose high and sheer
and above them steep slopes were overgrown with
larch and pine, making patterns of light and dark
green. The air was warm, bees and insects droned,
and as always in that place she felt small but safe.

A loud shout from one of the men in front made
her hurry on around a big outcrop of rock which
guarded the biggest and deepest pool in the river.
When she reached the narrow shingle beach
edging the pool she thought she noticed a movement on the opposite shore, a slight shaking of
the tiny birches, a ruffling of their heart-shaped
leaves as if a wind had passed over them on that
still and windless day.

'Come out of there, damn you!' roared Hamish
Taggart, who was head keeper of the estate.

There was no answer to his shout and no one
appeared on the opposite side of the pool, but
Hamish's own voice shouted back at him in
mocking echo.

'Who was it?' asked one of the other men. He was slight and slim, dressed in elegant tweeds, and his shiny black hair was brushed close to his narrow skull. His nose was hooked and his skin was sallow.

'A poacher,' growled Hamish, jerking his tweed cap forward over his eyes. A tall man, he had high square shoulders and grizzled grey hair and his tweeds had known many a soaking of fine Highland rain.

'How do you know?' asked another man. He was brown-haired and fair-skinned, and his grey-blue eyes glinted with excitement as they scanned the screen of birches on the opposite shore.

'He's left his weapon behind,' said Hamish, pointing to a ledge in the middle of the pool. 'Can't you see it?' On the ledge was a long wooden staff with a loop of wire at one end.

'What is a poacher?' asked the slim dark man. He spoke English with a strong foreign accent.

'Well now, it means someone who has no right to fish on the estate has been here and has taken a salmon from the pool using an illegal instrument, catching it by the tail with that loop of wire. He must have heard us coming. All I was seeing of him was a flash of silver in his hand which was the salmon and his bare feet and legs as he scrambled away up that bank,' replied Hamish.

'So.' The dark man's soft black eyes gleamed. 'He is a criminal, if he has no rights to fish on the estate. What is the worst you can do to him?'

'Have him fined, or put in jail if he can't be paying the fine,' said Hamish. 'But I doubt I'll be doing that now. He'll have got clean away while we've been standing here.'

He turned away and looked right at the woman. He gave a slight jerk of his head towards the opposite side of the pool and at once she began to walk back to the bank of shingle below the pool, hearing behind her the deep drone of Hamish's voice as he continued to explain to the other two men the complexities of fishing rights in the Highlands of Scotland.

Once she had crossed the bank of shingle she ducked under the branches of trees and began to climb a narrow path which twisted between broken rocks, overgrown with briar roses, black-berry vines and stunted birches, until she reached a small clearing high above the pool which was screened from the view of the men on the shore by a big boulder.

Behind the boulder a man was lying on his stomach and was watching the other men, who were just beginning to walk away down the course of the river, their departing footsteps crunching on shingle, their voices growing fainter. When she saw the man the woman stood still and stared down at him.

He was long and lean and was wearing grey corduroy trousers tucked into the tops of wel-lington boots, and under his heather-coloured sweater his shoulders were wide and flat. His red-dish-brown hair had the sheen of a chestnut's skin and was cut in an attractively shaggy style. He lay perfectly still until the other men could no longer be heard. Then with a quick lithe movement he got to his knees and began to stuff two pairs of boots and two pairs of socks into a canvas fishing bag.

It was while he was fastening the bag that he became aware of the woman's presence. Slowly his glance lifted from the bag and slowly it drifted upwards over her boots, up over her legs and body, up to her face. His eyes, which were a clear amber brown, widened slightly in surprise and he straightened up to his full height, slinging the strap of the bag over one of his shoulders. Shoving his hands into the pockets of his pants, he stood with his legs apart returning the woman's stare, his eyes now cold and blank.

'I've been looking at the heels of your boots for quite a while, Neil Dysart,' she said mockingly. 'Shame on you for poaching a salmon in daylight when the water in the pool is low! Anyone can catch a fish like that.'

'I'm not the poacher,' he replied coolly.

'Then who is? I can't see anyone else here.' She looked round the clearing deliberately.

'They've gone, and I'm not in the habit of betraying my friends,' he said curtly.

'They must be uncomfortable walking without their socks and boots,' she remarked dryly, her glance going to the bag. She looked back at him, a slight smile curving her lips. 'I do believe you've forgotten me,' she said softly. 'I'm Kirsty Whyte. My last name used to be Ure.'

His hard glance swept over her and a slight frown brought his heavy dark eyebrows together over the bridge of his thin aquiline nose.

'I remember you.' His glance raked her assessingly again. 'You look different,' he added bluntly.

'That's not surprising,' she said with a laugh. 'I'm nearly four years older than when we last met, and I do my hair differently.' She looked at him as frankly and as assessingly as he had looked at her. 'I can see a few changes in you, too,' she added lightly.

She didn't say what the changes were. Now thirty-four, going on for thirty-five, he was still straight and lean and his hair was still quite thick, springing back vigorously from the deep peak on his forehead. But the passage of time had left marks. His eyes no longer danced with a sparkle of mischief but were cold, clear pools of yellowish light. His high cheekbones looked strangely bruised as if he had been living too hard and his mouth was set in a taut controlled line.

'I suppose you're staying at the croft on Cairn Rua,' she said, feeling chilled suddenly by his unfriendly attitude.

'I am.'

'When did you come back?'

'A week ago.'

'Oh.' She was surprised, and annoyed too, because she hadn't been informed of his return and hadn't noticed any light at night beaming out from his cottage. 'You might have let me know.'

'I'd have got round to calling on you eventually,' he replied indifferently.

'I suppose you know that Alec died four months ago,' she said.

'I had heard,' he murmured laconically, and it seemed to her his eyes narrowed calculatingly as he continued to stare at her.

'Is your wife with you?' she asked as casually as she could feeling tension building up between them.

'No.' The curt dismissing negative showed her how he felt about her curiosity. It set her back, away from him. He looked in the direction of the dark yet light-reflecting pool which could just be seen over the tip of the boulder. 'Who was with Hamish, by the pool?' he asked.

'My brother Duncan, the new tenant of Balmore, and one of his security men.'

'Tenant?' he queried sharply, turning to her again. 'You're letting it?'

'Yes, as from the beginning of this month.'

'Just the house?'

'No, the whole estate. I'm hoping that if he likes living here he'll buy the place.'

For a moment he looked stunned, staring at her, his eyes wide. Then slowly they narrowed again and his mouth curved cynically.

'I never thought a day would come when Balmore would be let to a tenant with a view to selling it. Alec and his Whyte ancestors must be turning over in their graves,' he remarked jeeringly.

'I can't help that,' she retorted spiritedly, her blue eyes flashing. 'They don't have to maintain the place and I do. Alec left a mountain of debts when he died and his lawyer suggested that I let the house and the estate to raise money to pay off his creditors. It's taken me all this time to find someone willing and able to afford the rent, and if Sheikh Hussein al Dukar offers the right price I shall certainly sell it to him.'

'A sheikh, eh?' He stepped towards her, his eyes glinting with hostility. 'You'd dare to sell property, which was granted to the Whytes nearly five hundred years ago by a king of Scotland to an Arab oil millionaire?' he exclaimed. 'My God, I would never have believed you would have turned out to be so grasping!' His breath hissed as he drew it in. 'Surely the Balmore estate should be passed on to the next Whyte, to Alec's and your son.'

'Alec and I didn't have a son,' she said stiffly.

'Your daughter, then.'

'We didn't have any children,' she snapped back at him. 'The paralysis grew worse and made it impossible for him to . . . he wasn't able to. . . .' She broke off, the colour rising in her cheeks as she realised she was betraying to him the sterility of the two and a half years of her marriage to Alec.

'Then why the hell did you marry him?' his hostile eyes challenged her. 'Was it so you could become Lady Whyte of Balmore and inherit one of the biggest estates in the Highlands and then sell it?'

'No, it wasn't!' she retorted, her head up. 'I married Alec because I liked and respected him and because he was always kind to me.'

'And no doubt because you were sorry for him,' he sneered.

'Perhaps. I felt the least I could do in return for all the help and encouragement he'd given me was to help make the last years of his life a little easier and pleasanter. Isn't that what marriage is all about?'

'If you say so,' he drawled, his manner guarded again. 'So the fishing rights belong to an Arab while he's the tenant,' he went on. 'That's going to make a number of people who live on the estate unhappy, isn't it? I mean the owners of crofts like myself who have always had the privilege of fishing its streams and lochs when Alec and the other Whytes before him were lairds of Balmore.'

'Hussein is a very pleasant man, cultured and educated, and I think he'll make a good landlord, so you don't have to sneer at him,' she rebuked him.

'Maybe he's all you say he is, but I suspect he won't have any hesitation in punishing anyone who trespasses on his rights. He doesn't belong here, so he won't know to turn a blind eye when a local lad lifts a fish from his rivers.' He rubbed his chin and looked past her. 'I think I'd best be on my way to find my friends. They went down the river path and I wouldn't like them to run into Hamish and the Sheikh.'

'Hamish won't do anything to them,' she said, hurrying after him. 'In fact he sent me here to warn whoever was in hiding.'

He turned to look at her and the corners of his mouth tilted upwards in a grin.

'I see.' His eyes lost their coldness and began to dance with devilry, reminding her of other occasions when she had been with him, five years ago, and they had hidden together behind rocks or among bushes to avoid being caught by the headkeeper when they had helped themselves to a fish from a pool. 'The lads were only playing at being poachers,' he explained. 'They were trying to prove to me that they had the skill to lift a fish from low water under a bright sky. No one was more surprised than they were when they caught it. Of course if I'd known about the tenant I wouldn't have let them try.' He slanted her a curious glance. 'You seem to be very friendly with this Sheikh, calling him by his first name.'

'He asked me to,' she replied, tilting her chin.

Standing under the branches of the small birches they were much closer to each other than they had been. Hidden from view, shaded from the sun, the little glade was pervaded with intimate memories for Kirsty; memories of kisses and caresses they had exchanged on hot sunny afternoons; memories of passion which she had deliberately banished to the cellars of her mind but which were now breaking out of their imprisonment and storming her sensibilities. She wanted to cry out, to shout at Neil, and tell him to go away and leave her in peace. Instead she turned on her heel and began to walk swiftly down the twisting path towards the river.

'You should watch how you go,' behind her his voice taunted softly. 'You'll be spraining your ankle again if you're not careful, and we're a long way from the house. I wouldn't like to have to carry you there.'

The taunt was on target, reminding her of their first meeting, but instead of turning to retort Kirsty hurried on, slithering and sliding down the steep path until she reached the shingle bed below the big pools. Crossing it, she gained the riverside path and without looking back to see if Neil was following her she began to walk fast towards the loch.

It was a long time since she had felt like this, as if someone had taken hold of her and had shaken her roughly. But then Neil Dysart was the last person she had expected to see when she had climbed the rocks in search of a poacher. She shouldn't feel anything, she argued with herself. After all, she wasn't twenty-one any longer. She had been married and widowed, so she should be able to take an unexpected meeting with a former lover in her stride.

Kirsty's stride faltered in spite of her and she slowed down. Lifting her head, she looked across the loch to the slopes of Cairn Rua. Under the direct rays of the sun the spread of the moors glowed red and the rocky summit above them glinted fierily, giving the hill its name of Red Rock. Below the moors, half buried among trees and bushes, the walls of a cottage gleamed white and its windows winked with golden light.

It had been evening and the loch had been shining with a silvery light of its own as the moors had darkened to purple when she had limped to the door of that distant cottage almost five years ago. Out for a walk by herself, she had inadvertently stepped into an unseen rabbit hole and had sprained her ankle. She had noticed the crofter's house with a sense of relief and had knocked on its door confidently, knowing that the people of the Scottish Highlands are among the most generous and hospitable people in the world and would assuredly find a way to help her return to the house where she had been staying.

But the door had remained shut and she had begun to think there was no one at home when a movement to her left had startled her. Turning quickly, she had found herself face to face with a tall man who had been carrying a fishing rod.

In the mysterious violet-tinted dusk which had filled the flower-scented garden of the cottage they had stared at each other in silent surprise. He had moved and had spoken first, coming towards her with his gold-flecked amber-brown eyes gazing into hers incredulously.

'Who are you? And what are you doing here?' he had whispered.

As if she had been struck dumb she had only been able to continue to stare at him, falling in love with him on sight, seeing in his tall wide-shouldered figure, proud aquiline features and plume of chestnut brown hair the embodiment of all her romantic fantasies. He had repeated the questions in another language and the spell in which she had been caught temporarily had been broken. She had laughed and had shaken her head.

'I don't have the Gaelic. I'm not a Highlander,' she had replied. 'I'm Kirsty Ure and I'm working at Balmore Lodge for the summer. I've hurt my ankle, so I was knocking at the door thinking I might get help. Do you live here?'

'For this summer only,' he had answered briefly, and dropping his fishing rod he had gone down on one knee before her, and immediately she had been caught up again in a spell of romance, seeing him as a clan chieftain returned from the wars to pay homage to his lady. With both hands he had felt her left ankle, and his touch had been both gentle and confident.

'It does seem to be swollen,' he had said, and had straightened up. 'Let me help you into the house and I'll have a proper look at it.'

Glad of his support, she had entered the living room of the cottage and had sat down on an old ladderbacked chair beside an open hearth built of granite blocks in which a fire had been laid in the dog grate but not lit. Neil had touched lighted matches to the wicks of the two brass Aladdin oil lamps, which had been the only form of lighting in the house, and setting one of them on a small table near the chair he had knelt on one knee before her again. Lifting her left foot on to his other bent knee, he had removed her shoe and her sock. Against the bruised skin in front of the ankle bone his fingers had probed searchingly.

'Nothing broken,' he had said, lowering her foot and glancing up at her.

'How do you know?' she had challenged, aware of a strange quivering excitement fluttering along her nerves.

'I ought to know,' he had replied, flashing her a smile. 'I'm an orthopaedic surgeon. I'll bandage it for you. It needs support and you shouldn't walk on it for a while.'

'But how am I going to get back to the Lodge? I can't hop all the way,' she had complained.

'I'll take you there in my car. It's parked at the back of the house.' Again he had smiled at her. 'It isn't a Rolls-Royce and it isn't new, but it goes.' He had stood up and had gone over to an old dresser to take something from a drawer. 'Are you a friend of Sir Alec Whyte's?' he had asked casually as he had come back to her carrying a pink elastic bandage.

'No. I'm working for him. I'm studying Biology and Forestry. He advertised for a student to help him with the book he's writing about the natural history of the Highlands. I answered the advert and got the job,' she had explained while he had bandaged her ankle swiftly and expertly. 'I'll be here until the university term begins.'

'How long before you graduate?' he had asked.

'I have another year's study to do,' she had replied.

'And then?'

'I'll hope to get a job in Nature Conservancy or on an estate like Balmore. Or I might go abroad.'

By then he had been on both his knees and his hands had been resting on the arms of the old chair. Slowly he had leaned towards her, his hands sliding along the arms until she had been trapped against the back of the chair.

'You have the bluest eyes I've ever seen,' he had murmured, and his own eyes had glittered with a rich tawny light like topazes. 'They're as blue as speedwells, the tiny flowers which grow among the grasses at the edge of the forests. And when I first saw you standing at my doorway in the twilight with your hair hanging like a wimple about your face I thought for a moment you were the ghost of some Highland lady come to haunt this place.'

'And when I saw you with your rod in your hand I thought you were a clan chieftain with your sword, come to claim me as your lady,' she had whispered back.

'It seems we share similar fantasies,' he had replied, and as a strange indefinable longing to share more with him had swept over her she had placed her hands on his shoulders and had lifted her face to his. He had hesitated, his eyes clouding with doubt, then with a sound, half groan and half sigh, he had bent his head towards hers.

When his lips had touched hers she had shivered, not with cold but with delight, because his lips had been cool and firm yet sweet and seductive, just as she had always imagined her lover's lips would be. His tongue had flickered tantalisingly against her lips, and she had been surprised and a little shocked by its intimate touch and by the sensations it had aroused in her, because no man had ever kissed her like that before. Slowly but willingly her lips had parted, learning from his. The kiss had deepened and her arms had gone round him to hold him closely. . . .

A whaup called with sudden sharp sadness as it winged its way above the moors, and Kirsty was jolted back into the present to find herself at the place where the path met the road which curved beside the loch, the parting of the ways for her and Neil. She would take the road which sloped up to Balmore Lodge and he would take the lower part of the road to walk the mile or so to the other shore and up Cairn Rua to his cottage. The distant hill, the glinting house, the shining loch all swam into focus before her eyes again, but her skin was filmed with sweat, her mouth was dry and her heart was pounding as remembered passion continued to pulse through her.

Her hands clenched at her sides, she was cursing Neil Dysart silently for having come back and was turning to walk up the road when he spoke behind her.

'Kirsty.'

His hand touched her arm. Immediately she flinched away and swung round to face him, her chin up, her face pale and stiff, her eyelids drooping haughtily over her eyes.

'Well?' she snapped. 'What is it now?'

Faced with her hostility he changed. His eyes went blank, his nostrils flared slightly and his mouth twisted cynically.

'I was only going to ask you where you're living while the Sheikh is staying in the Lodge,' he said curtly.

'I'm living in the factor's house,' she replied. 'Alec hired me to be the factor of the estate after I graduated and I continued to do the job after we were married. I'm still doing it, and if I sell the estate to Hussein I'll make it a condition of the sale that he employs me as his factor.'

His eyes narrow, their expression hostile, he looked beyond her at the house whose pale walls sparkled through the green foliage of shrubs and trees.

'You mustn't sell it,' he said harshly, glaring at her. 'You mustn't sell it to the Sheikh.'

'I can do what I like with it,' she retorted. 'And perhaps I should remind you that you have no right to tell me what to do with Balmore—no right at all. Alec left it to me and once I've got probate it will be mine to do what I like with.'

'And I have to remind you, Lady Whyte, that I have the same rights as anyone else who holds a croft on the estate. I have the right to object if you dare to sell the property to a foreigner,' he retorted.

'Then maybe I won't sell,' she said lightly and mockingly. 'Maybe I'll marry Hussein instead and use his millions to turn Balmore into the show-place of the Western Highlands.'

'You'd marry for money?' he exclaimed, frowning at her.

'Why not? You did. So why shouldn't I?'

If her taunt about his marriage to the daughter of a wealthy American business tycoon found its mark he didn't show it but continued to stare at her in a cold calculating way that made her feel uneasy.

'No sheikh is going to be master of Balmore while I'm alive,' he muttered threateningly.

'My goodness, you sound as if you're declaring war on Hussein!' she said flippantly, but she backed away from him, disturbed by the flicker of violence now showing in his eyes. More than ever he reminded her of a fiercely proud Highland chieftain determined to defend his heritage to the death.

'I am,' he replied succintly.

They stared at each other like enemies; enemies who had once been lovers. Searching his taut angry face, Kirsty wondered if he remembered what had happened between them four years ago and guessed that what had meant so much to her when she had been twenty-one, vulnerable and a little naïve, in love for the first time, had meant little, possibly nothing, to him. For him she had been merely a passing fancy, a brief summer affair in which he had indulged his own physical desires, an entertaining deviation from the path he had been following at the time in pursuit of a career as a surgeon and of a wealthy wife.

Footsteps sounded on the road behind her. Neil looked past her. She turned to see who was coming. Her older brother Duncan appeared round a bend walking fast. His usually good-humoured face was wearing an anxious frown.

'Och, here you are,' he said, coming up to her. 'I was just looking for you. There's hell to pay up at the Lodge.' He became aware of Neil and glanced at him curiously. 'I don't think we've met,' he said bluntly.

'Neil Dysart,' said Neil, holding out his right hand.

'Duncan Ure, art dealer.' Duncan's curiosity deepened. 'You look familiar, for some reason.

You're not related to the artist Morag Dysart, by any chance?'

'She was my mother,' said Neil.

'Well now, if this isn't a coincidence!' exclaimed Duncan. 'Only this morning I was looking at two watercolours painted by her, both of them views of the scenery around here. I found them in a room in the turret. Both of them are dedicated to someone called Ian.'

'Sir Ian Whyte,' murmured Neil. 'He was my father.'

'Good God!' said Duncan excitedly. 'That's it. You're like him about the eyes and the hair grows in the same way. Of course,' he added with a grin, 'I've only seen his portrait.'

'Where? Where have you seen it?' demanded Kirsty.

'In the turret room.' Duncan jerked his head towards the house. 'It was with the watercolours. What's the matter with you? Didn't Alec ever tell you he had a half-brother?'

'No. No one ever told me. You didn't tell me.' Kirsty glared accusingly at Neil.

'I thought you knew. I thought Alec had told you,' he said coolly. 'Not that he had any reason to acknowledge my existence. As far as he was concerned I was born the wrong side of the blanket.'

'You should have told me,' was all she could say. He shrugged indifferently and turned to Duncan.

'What's going on at the Lodge?' he asked.

'Och, that Sheikh of yours is going to be more

trouble than he's worth, Kirsty,' Duncan grumbled.

'Why? What's he done? What's happened?' she demanded. She was feeling more than shaken now. She was feeling as if she had been turned upside down and she couldn't stop staring at Neil, who was deliberately ignoring her and looking at Duncan. Why had Alec never told her that Neil was his illegitimate half-brother? Why had he kept her in ignorance? Why?

'That big bodyguard of his, the one who walked up to the pool with us, spotted two lads crossing the river. They were without socks and shoes and had obviously been fishing.'

'Did they have a salmon?' asked Kirsty sharply, dragging her gaze away from Neil's aquiline features to look at her brother and attend better to what he was telling her.

'No. They had only fishing rods. I pointed out to the Sheikh that they didn't have a fish when he insisted they must be the poachers, but he wouldn't listen. Anyway, to cut the story short, he had them brought to the Lodge, and because they refused to answer his questions or to give their names he's locked them up in one of the garages until the police arrive to deal with them.'

'Has he called the police yet?' snapped Neil sharply.

'Not yet. Hamish and I managed to put him off by telling him that Kirsty should call the police because she is the factor as well as the owner of the estate, then I came to look for her,' said Duncan. He turned again to Kirsty. 'You're going to have difficulty in talking him out of bringing the police in. He's determined that they should be punished for what he calls "their serious crime against his person".'

'Oh, no!' groaned Kirsty, feeling suddenly irritated with the antics of supposedly adult men. 'This is all your fault,' she complained, swinging round to glare at Neil, but he wasn't there. Not by a quiver of a leaf did the shrubs betray that he had pushed his way through them. Shading her eyes against the glare of the sun, she looked down the road, but he hadn't gone that way either. Nor was he on the shore of the loch. She looked at Duncan.

'Where did he go?' she demanded angrily.

'How should I know?' His blue-grey eyes were bland, and she guessed he knew exactly which way Neil had gone. He had guessed also that Neil had something to do with the poachers and with typical Scottish clannishness he had closed ranks with his own countrymen to present a united front to the 'incomer' who was Hussein. 'Are you coming to see the Sheikh now?' he asked smoothly.

'Oh, I suppose so,' she snapped, wiping her brow with the back of one hand in an unconsciously weary gesture. Duncan's face softened and he pulled her arm through his as they began to walk up the road to the house.

'You got a shock just now when Dysart admitted to being Sir Ian's illegitimate son, didn't you?' he said.

'Yes. I wonder why Alec never told me?'

'Well, you know what old Alec was alike—a bit

of a puritan. I don't suppose he really approved
of his father and was ashamed of the old man's
behaviour with the opposite sex. He probably
didn't want you to know Sir Ian had a fairly torrid
love affair with Morag Dysart. I expect that's why
her paintings are hidden in the turret room. You
know, they should fetch a good price. Her paintings have become very popular recently. Some of
the other original paintings in the house are worth
a lot too.'

'Thanks for coming up from Edinburgh and
looking at them,' said Kirsty, giving his arm an
affectionate squeeze. 'I wish you'd brought Jean
and the girls with you, then you could all have
stayed for a few days with me. There's just one
thing that puzzles me. How did you know there
were some paintings in the turret room?'

'Mary Taggart, the housekeeper, told me when
I asked her if she knew of any paintings other
than those on show in the gallery and the lounge,'
he replied, giving her a sideways glance. 'When
did you first meet Dysart?'

'When I first came here, five years ago. He was
living then in the croft which had belonged to his
mother. Soon after I met him he left and went to
New York to work with a famous surgeon there.
He married the heiress to the Gow millions.'

'*Whew!* He did well for himself, didn't he?'
remarked Duncan. 'What's he doing back here?'

'I don't know. He didn't tell me.'

'Perhaps he's going to contest Alec's will. As
Sir Ian's younger son he might think he has more
right to the property than you have.'

'That did cross my mind,' said Kirsty with a sigh. 'But I don't see how he can contest the will. I mean, he said himself he was born the wrong side of the blanket, so he can't really prove he's Sir Ian's son, can he? I don't think there's anything he can do to claim Balmore as his.'

'I wouldn't be too sure about that,' warned Duncan thoughtfully. 'I got the impression he's a man who'll fight for what he believes is his and what he believes is right, regardless of consequences.'

CHAPTER TWO

BALMORE LODGE was a simple but elegant two-storey house built from limestone quarried from a nearby hillside. Mullioned windows glinted on either side of a gracious front entrance and at one end of the building there was a round tower or turret with a pointed roof.

In front of the house a smooth green lawn rolled down to the shore of the loch. At the back of the house, enclosed by tall hedges, were the famous gardens where Sir Alec Whyte had once supervised the cultivation of many species of plants. Behind the gardens a wood of mixed coniferous and deciduous trees climbed a hillside. Above the trees the moors, a mosaic of purple bell-heather just in bloom, black bog and green bracken, spread, rolled and lifted to lavender grey rocks.

Duncan and Kirsty went straight to the courtyard beside the house and he pointed to the old stable buildings which had long been used as garages. Standing on either side of the double doors of one of the garages were two swarthy-skinned, black-haired Arabs, dressed neatly in white shirts and light grey suits.

'The lads are in that one,' Duncan whispered.

'Did you see them?' asked Kirsty.

'Of course I did. Both of them were about twenty-five or six and both of them were stubborn

Scots, refusing to speak. I warned the Sheikh that he was breaking the law by detaining them, but he wouldn't listen to me or to Hamish. Maybe he'll listen to you.'

'They're friends of Neil's,' Kirsty told him.

'Then they're probably medics; perhaps house surgeons from some hospital,' Duncan guessed.

'He said they were only playing at poaching. You're quite sure they didn't have a salmon?'

'Quite sure.'

'Then even if the police are called in nothing can be done to them without evidence,' mused Kirsty. 'I'll go and tell Hussein that. We can't expect him to know or understand the law of the land yet. He hasn't been in Scotland for very long.'

They entered the house by a side door and walked along a passage to the big entrance hall which was panelled in golden pinewood and had a wide staircase going up to a gallery where paintings hung. Outside the double carved pinewood doors of the lounge another Arab stood on guard. Kirsty asked him if she could see the Sheikh. The man nodded, asked her to wait, opened the door, entered the room and closed the door behind him.

'All this security and formality makes me angry,' muttered Duncan. 'Anyone would think you were a visitor in your own house!'

'I am while Hussein is paying rent for it,' Kirsty replied.

'But why does he need so many bodyguards?'

'He has to be careful about the people who

approach him. His father was assassinated only a few months ago by a young terrorist who was allowed to enter the palace in Dukar somehow. Since then there has also been an attempt on Hussein's life,' explained Kirsty. 'It isn't fun being wealthy or the ruler of a country these days, with so many terrorists roaming the world.'

The door opened again and the Arab security man indicated that Kirsty could enter the wide, high-ceilinged room. As soon as he saw her Hussein sprang to his feet from the chair behind the delicate antique writing desk where he had been sitting and writing. He came across to her, his right hand outstretched in greeting as if he hadn't seen her for a long time.

'Ah, Christina, I'm glad you have returned at last. Has Duncan told you we have caught the poachers?' he said.

'Yes, he has.'

'And now we must punish them.' Hussein's eyes gleamed with a cold cruel light.

Although she knew he was a couple of years younger than she was Kirsty always felt he was older. There was about him an indefinable sadness, as if he had been forced to grow up too quickly; as if he had had no time in his life for mischief or the typical wild oats behaviour of most young-men. She knew he was going to have great difficulty in understanding what she had to tell him about the easygoing relationship that had always existed in Scotland over hundreds of years between clan chieftain and clansman, between landowner and crofter. Equality between men, equality between men and women too, was something Hussein had never known.

'We can't punish them,' she said.

'But they have done wrong,' he exclaimed. 'They have broken the law and stolen a fish from the river.'

'How do you know they've stolen a fish? Did they have a fish when Ahmed caught them?'

'No. But your head keeper saw one of them leaving the pool and they had no shoes and socks on,' he replied sharply, frowning at her. 'I would like you to call the police now, if you please, Christina,' he continued autocratically. 'I want them arrested.'

'The police will only arrest them if there's some evidence that the young men you've locked in the garage have stolen a fish,' she explained as patiently as she could. 'But there is no evidence. There's only Hamish's word that he saw a man leaving the pool in a hurry. That's what's called hearsay, and it isn't enough. The police won't accept it and they won't make an arrest.'

'It is very puzzling.' He shook his head from side to side.

'And when the police know that you've forcibly detained two men and have locked them up your bodyguards could be charged with assault and you could be charged with illegally arresting them.'

'I do not understand,' he said, and shook his head again. 'I thought the police in this country existed to enforce the law of the land.'

'They do. But the laws are made to protect the

citizens ... *all* the citizens,' Kirsty was saying when there was a commotion at the door. One of the security men who had been standing guard outside the garage doors came into the room. He came right up to Hussein, salaamed briefly and began to talk very fast in Arabic. Hussein listened attentively, his expression varying from irritation to anger chasing across his narrow sallow face.

'They have escaped!' he exclaimed, turning to Kirsty when the bodyguard finished explaining. 'And they have stolen my Rolls-Royce. We must go after them. Ahmed, my man here, will go after them. Please, Christina, will you lend him your car?'

'Yes, yes ... of course. The keys are in the glove compartment,' said Kirsty. She glanced appealingly at Duncan. 'Please go with Ahmed,' she whispered. 'I don't want any more violence. I wouldn't like anyone to be hurt.'

'All right,' he said. 'I'll go. Although how we're expected to catch up with a Rolls-Royce in your beaten-up old Sunbeam I don't know,' he added grumblingly.

He left the room with Ahmed and Hussein turned to Kirsty.

'How can this have happened?' demanded Hussein.

'I don't know,' she said with a sigh. But she had a good idea that Neil Dysart was the mastermind behind the escape of the poachers, remembering how he had disappeared so suddenly after Duncan had told her how the poachers had been caught and locked up.

'Ahmed is very strong. They could never get past him,' mused Hussein. 'He says they must have been able to get from the garage where they were locked up to the garage where my car was. How could they do that? Do you know?'

'If they could have got up into the hayloft through the trapdoor they could have reached the other garages. The loft runs the full length of the stables above them,' replied Kirsty.

'Then they must know the buildings very well, better than my men know them,' remarked Hussein shrewdly.

Or they had help from someone outside who had known the buildings well, thought Kirsty. Someone like Neil. Or had Hamish helped them? No, the head keeper wouldn't have done anything to help anyone whom he suspected of trying to poach one of his salmon.

'So now you do have good reason to phone the police,' Hussein said. 'My car has been stolen. Do you know the number of the police station?'

'The nearest station is in Fort William, about forty miles away from here,' said Kirsty, going over to the writing desk. 'The number is in the directory.'

'Please find it for me,' ordered Hussein, and for one wild rebellious moment she was tempted to refuse, to tell him to find the number himself, because she wasn't one of his servants to be bossed about in such a peremptory manner. Then she remembered she needed the money he was paying for renting the estate and she subdued her rebellious feelings quickly. Taking the directory out of the desk drawer, she looked up the number and wrote it down on a pad of paper for him. He looked at it, looked at the telephone, then looked at her. A slight diffident smile curved his lips, making him look younger.

'Please, Christina, will you phone them for me?' he asked, and the autocratic manner had gone. He was appealing to her charmingly. 'I have difficulty in understanding what your fellow countrymen say over the phone. Their accent is so different.'

'Oh, very well.' Kirsty picked up the receiver and dialled. In a few seconds she was talking to a police sergeant. She explained what had happened and listened to the questions he asked her. At first he sounded very sceptical when she told him that the Rolls-Royce belonging to His Excellency the Sheikh Hussein al Dukar had been stolen, but he seemed more disposed to believe her when she provided him with the registration number of the car.

'Ye wouldn't have any idea now which way they were travelling, would ye?' asked the sergeant.

'Well, there's only one way to go from Balmore estate and that is to the village of Balvaig. From there they could go either north to Ullapool or south to Fort William.'

'Thank you. I'll inform any of our men who happen to be on duty in the vicinity to keep a look out for it. That's all I can do.'

'Please let me know as soon as you hear anything of it,' said Kirsty.

'Just let me have your name and phone number and I'll do that,' replied the sergeant.

She supplied the information and rang off. Turning to Hussein, she told him what the sergeant had said.

'And that's all we can do for now,' she added. 'I'm really sorry this has happened, your Excellency. . . .'

'Hussein, please, Christina,' he pleaded.

'But if you hadn't decided to take the law into your own hands. . . .'

'They wouldn't have taken the law into their hands,' he finished for her dryly. 'I understand now, I think,' he went on in a low voice. 'It is not your fault. There is so much I have to learn about this country and about the estate. But you can teach me much. I hope we become good friends while I stay here.' He moved towards her, smiling a little, his dark eyes warm. 'Would you like for us to be friends?'

His appeal for friendship touched her generous heart. She saw suddenly how lonely he was in the high position into which he had been thrust by the unexpected death of his father.

'Of course I would like to be your friend,' she replied impulsively.

'I have never been able to have a woman friend,' he continued. 'When my father was alive he forbade me to have women friends.'

'But surely he wanted you to marry and to have children,' she exclaimed.

'Oh yes, he wanted that for me. But he would only approve of marriage to women of my own country, simple girls who would accept without question a position in my harem in the Islamic tradition. It was the Western women I met when I was a student in Paris and then at Oxford that he worried about. He was afraid I might fall in love with a Christian foreigner and want to marry her.' His charming, shy smile appeared. 'But until now I haven't had any desire to marry. What about you, Christina? You are young to have been left a widow. Would you ever consider marrying again?'

'I might, if the right man came along,' she replied noncommittally.

'And how will you recognise the right man?' he queried, laughing a little. 'Do you have a list of the qualities he must possess? If so please tell me what they are and then I'll be able to tell whether I have them or not.'

'No, I don't have a list, and even if I did, I wouldn't tell you,' she replied teasingly, feeling lighthearted suddenly. It seemed a long time since she had been able to indulge in such a conversation with a young man. Her marriage to Alec, who had been so much older than she, had tended to cut her off from relationships with her peer group. 'You'll just have to take your chance with all the others.'

'So,' Hussein's smile widened into a grin which showed his beautiful teeth, 'you have many admirers? I am not surprised. You are very pretty, with your pink and white skin, your black hair and your blue eyes. But I also admire your competence in looking after this huge estate. And your independence of spirit, your refusal to be domineered over is extremely attractive to me. I'm glad I have competition. It always brings out the best in me, and I'll take my chances as you suggest. To begin with I'd like to invite you to dinner here in the Lodge this evening. Some friends of mine from France will be arriving in half an hour and I'd like them to meet you. Will you come, please, Christina?'

'I'd like to. But Duncan is staying the night with me and he'll be expecting me to provide his dinner,' she said.

'Then bring him to dinner with you. He can entertain us with his opinions of the paintings he has been evaluating for you and we shall have a very pleasant party,' replied Hussein, his mood more lively and more cheerful than she had ever known it to be. 'I'll expect you both at about seven o'clock.'

It was almost six-thirty and Kirsty was changing in her bedroom at the factor's house when she heard Duncan come in. He called to her and with a last glance at her reflection in the mirror she left the bedroom and went downstairs. In the small hallway his blue-grey glance took in the dress she was wearing. A soft shade of blue, it had a pleated skirt and a softly draped bodice with a frill at the neckline and frills at the cuffs of the long sleeves.

'Why are you all dressed up?' he asked with brotherly directness.

'We're invited to have dinner with Hussein at the Lodge. He expects us at seven. Did you find the Rolls?'

'No.' His glance was derisive. 'Did you expect us to?'

'Which way did you go?'

'Beyond Balvaig and then part way along the road to Fort William. Then your car started to behave badly. It took me a while to get it going again.'

'What was wrong with it?'

'Och, this and that,' Duncan said evasively. 'By the time it was going again Ahmed agreed with me that there was no point in pursuing the Rolls, so we came back here.' He glanced down at his hands. The fingers were marked with motor oil. 'If we're expected at seven at the Lodge I'd better get cleaned up,' he added, turning towards the stairs.

'Now wait a minute, Duncan Ure,' said Kirsty, purposefully stepping in front of him. She could tell by his blandness that he had been up to some sort of mischief. 'I don't believe there was anything wrong with my car. It had its monthly check-up only last week. I think you pretended there was something wrong with it.'

'Now why would I be doing something like that, Kirsty?' he asked, rounding his eyes in an expression of innocence.

'Because you didn't want to give chase to the poachers that's why,' she accused.

'Och, I was never able to get away with lying to you,' he grumbled. 'All right—there wasn't anything wrong with the car, but I wasn't going to chase the Rolls as far as Fort William when I knew damned well it was still here on the estate.'

'Still here?' she gasped in puzzlement. 'How do you know?'

'When I left here with Ahmed in the Sunbeam I noticed the Rolls climbing the road to the croft on Cairn Rua,' he said.

'Neil took them to his cottage?' she exclaimed.

'So, like me, you guessed Dysart sprang the lads free from the garage,' said Duncan with a pleased and knowing grin. 'I didn't tell Ahmed I'd spotted the Rolls and I drove part way to Fort William to give the lads long enough to collect their gear and be on their way.'

'Conspirator!' Kirsty hissed at him, but he only grinned again. 'Oh, you and Neil Dysart make a nice pair of mischief-makers!'

'I agree with you,' he said equably. 'And I think we'd have done well together dodging the Redcoats after the Forty-Five Rebellion,' he added. 'My trick to divert Ahmed and the other bodyguard worked too. We were just coming back through Balvaig when a small car passed us going the other way. I recognised the driver as one of the poachers, but Ahmed and the other fellow never noticed them. They'll be well on their way past Fort William by now.'

'Thank God,' said Kirsty with feeling. 'I wasn't looking forward to hearing from the police that they'd found the Rolls and had arrested the thieves.'

'You didn't phone the police?' exclaimed Duncan, scowling fiercely at her.

'I had to—Hussein insisted. And it did look as if his car had been stolen, didn't it?' she retorted defensively. 'Where is it now?'

'Still at Dysart's cottage, I suppose,' said

Duncan, beginning to go up the stairs. 'I expect he'll return it sooner or later. At least his friends got away.' With one hand on the banister he turned to look down at her, suddenly very much her bossy older brother. 'Now you're not to tell Hussein about any of this, Kirsty, do you hear?'

'I hear,' she replied with a sigh of exasperation. 'Hurry up and wash, Hussein has guests from France and he wants us to meet them.'

The elegant oval dining room of the Lodge looked its best that evening with candlelight gleaming softly on Royal Doulton china, fine silver cutlery and delicate Stuart crystal. If Hussein was still worried about the theft of his car he made no mention of it to his French guests, Monsieur and Madame Delacroix and their daughter Camille, and neither Kirsty nor Duncan made reference to the afternoon's events. The evening passed pleasantly with good food, good wine and stimulating conversation, and at eleven o'clock Kirsty and Duncan said goodnight to their host and his guests and returned to the factor's house.

'A very interesting day,' remarked Duncan with a yawn. 'I'd have liked to have gone over to have a word with Dysart to tell him his friends got away, but I think I'll leave you to pass on that piece of information.' He glanced sideways at Kirsty. 'I suppose you'll be seeing him.'

'I might,' said Kirsty shortly. 'Are you going to tell me how much you think the paintings might bring before you go?'

'I'll make out a list of them with the prices I

think they'll fetch and leave it with you.' He gave her another thoughtful glance. 'You know, it would be a nice gesture on your part to give those two Dysart paintings to Neil.'

'I'll think about it.' She spoke shortly again.

'You don't like him, do you?'

'Don't like whom?' she queried, being deliberately obtuse.

'Neil Dysart.'

'Not at the moment I don't,' she replied, going towards the stairs. 'One way and another he's caused me a lot of trouble today.'

'And it's my guess he and other local people are going to cause you more trouble while this place is let to the Sheikh,' Duncan warned seriously. 'It's a pity you didn't think of selling some of the paintings or the antiques before you leased Balmore to a tenant. They might have brought in enough money to pay part of Alec's debts.'

'Letting Balmore was a much quicker way of raising money,' Kirsty argued. 'Hussein has paid six months' rent in advance. What time are you leaving in the morning?' she added.

'About nine.'

'We'll have breakfast at eight, then. Goodnight.'

' 'Night, Kirsty.'

She didn't sleep well that night. The unexpected meeting with Neil, his sardonic confession that he was Sir Ian Whyte's illegitimate son and his mischievous rescue of his friends from the garage had set her nerves on edge, so that every time she started to slip into sleep thoughts of him would prod her cruelly into wakefulness again. He had leapt back into her life to torment her and she knew she wouldn't regain her peace of mind until she confronted him again and demanded why he had come back to Balmore.

Next morning Duncan was unkind enough to comment on the lines sleeplessness had scored under her eyes, but before he left he gave her a hug and a kiss.

'Let me know if you want to sell any of the paintings,' he said.

'I will,' she promised. 'And next time you come bring Jean and the girls and stay longer.'

She was clearing the breakfast table when she heard him come back into the house. She hurried out into the hall thinking he had forgotten something. Standing just inside the front door, he was grinning delightedly.

'The Rolls is back,' he said. 'I told you he'd bring it back—must have brought it at dead of night when there was no one around to see or hear him. The Sheikh and his bodyguard are dancing around it, exclaiming and looking for damage.'

'I'd better go and have a word with Hussein,' said Kirsty, whipping off her apron. 'And I'll have to phone the police to ask them to call off the search.'

Although he was pleased that his favourite toy had been returned to him unscratched Hussein was plainly puzzled by its stealthy reappearance and had soon come to the conclusion that the two poachers must have had a friend living on the estate who had helped them to escape.

'I shall interview everyone who lives on the estate,' he announced to Kirsty after she had phoned the police at Fort William. 'Please will you invite all of the people who work for you or who have farms or crofts to come here tomorrow afternoon for tea? It will be an "at home" party and will give me the opportunity to meet them and for them to meet me. A good idea, don't you think?'

'Yes, it's a good idea,' agreed Kirsty cautiously. 'I'll go and find Hamish now and ask him to pass the invitation on. What time would you like everyone to come?'

'At three o'clock. And if it is a fine day we'll have tea served on the terrace.' Hussein smiled with pleasure. 'I like to entertain,' he confided in her. 'Especially do I like to entertain people who work for me. I enjoy being . . . what do you call it?' He snapped his fingers together.

'A benefactor?' she suggested.

'Exactly.' He beamed at her. 'I like to be kind, to do good, and I can afford to.'

'But don't you think it's rather hypocritical to give a party . . . or to do good . . . just so you can find out who borrowed your car to help the young men to get away?' she argued.

'Can you suggest any other way I can find out?'

'No, not really. But supposing you do find out who took the car. What will you do to him?'

'I don't know,' he said with a laugh. 'It will depend on what he is like.' His eyes narrowed.

'You look worried, Christina. Is it possible you know the culprit and are afraid I might have him put in jail?'

'I'm afraid of what you might do to whoever borrowed your car, but not on his behalf. I'm afraid that if you punish him severely you will become unpopular with the people who live on the estate and that they will then make your stay here very uncomfortable,' she said very seriously. 'And I wouldn't like that to happen to you.'

'Thank you, Christina,' he said, coming to stand close to her, so close that she could smell his strongly scented aftershave lotion. 'I am glad that it is on my behalf you are afraid.' He reached out and took her hand in his and raised it to his lips. 'Already we are becoming friends,' he whispered, his dark eyes glowing sensuously as he fondled her hands with both of his. 'I wish we could. . . .' He broke off as the door behind her opened. He dropped her hand, his head tipped back haughtily and he spoke sharply in Arabic to the man who had entered.

'Excuse me,' said Kirsty, glad of a chance to escape from what might have become a difficult situation to handle, and with a nod and a smile at the security man Ahmed she left the room.

She found Hamish in the byre at the back of the garages. He wasn't impressed when she told him about the tea party.

'Ach, I'm thinking no one will be wanting to have tea with yon Sheikh,' he complained.

'And I'm thinking they will want to have tea with him out of sheer curiosity, if nothing else,'

Kirsty retorted. 'Now you be sure to tell every-one.'

'Ye want me to tell himself over at Cairn Rua?' he asked, cocking a shrewd grey eye at her.

'No, I'll tell Mr Dysart,' she said coolly. 'By the way, why didn't you tell me he'd come back?'

'Well now, ye might say it slipped my mind,' drawled Hamish, looking past her, his eyes taking on the distant dreamy expression that meant he wasn't telling the truth.

'Do you know why he's come back?' she asked sharply. In all the time she had lived at Balmore she had never been able to get a straight answer out of Hamish, yet of all the people who lived and worked on the estate he probably knew the most about the Whyte family. He probably knew that Neil was Sir Ian Whyte's younger son, but he would never have admitted to anyone that he knew.

'Ach, he's come for a wee bit of a holiday, I'm thinking,' he replied, still vague. Then he looked at her suddenly, his expression no longer dreamy but sharp with hostility. 'And why shouldn't he come here? The croft is his. He inherited it from his mother. And he has as much right as anyone to live on the estate; more right than some.' He gave her another piercing glance, then hunching one shoulder, turned away from her. 'Ach, well, if I'm going to be delivering that invitation to everyone I'd best be off. It's likely to be taking me all day to get round the estate, so it is. As if I didn't have enough of me own work to do.'

He clumped away across the courtyard. For a

few moments Kirsty stood thinking. The sun was growing warmer. It was going to be another fine day. She glanced towards the loch. Blue, satin-smooth, it stretched away to the slopes of Cairn Rua. Slowly she began to walk out of the court-yard to the road.

She should really have gone the other way, back to the factor's house to attend to estate business, but it was too pleasant a morning to spend indoors. She would walk round the head of the loch and find out how the stand of pines and birches which had been planted the previous year on the lower slopes of Cairn Rua were progress-ing.

The road was dry and dusty, splashed with bright yellow light where the sun shone through the foliage of the trees which edged it on her right. To her left the loch dimpled and glittered among the reeds and a heron, disturbed by her approach, took to the air with a great flapping of its wings.

How often she had walked this way that August four years ago! Every afternoon she had come. She had walked slowly as she was walking now, taking pleasure in all that was around her; in the play of light and shadow, the flash of brilliant blue as a kingfisher dived to the loch, the soft gurgle of the water as it lapped among the reeds. Sometimes she had stopped to examine and admire some wild flowers growing in the grasses at the side of the road, just as she was stopping now. But wherever she had looked her glance had always been drawn back to the slopes of the hill before her; to the white walls of the small cottage glinting in the sunlight as they were glinting now, beckoning to her.

Her meetings with Neil had happened every day for over four weeks and had apparently been accidental, although she had always walked this way on purpose, hoping to meet him. She had done all the seeking out. He had never come looking for her. Yet when they had met on the hillside she had always been so shy and tonguetied in his presence that he had then taken the initiative and had made the next moves.

Young and hopeful, she had really believed he had been as emotionally involved with her as she had been with him. She had expected their affair to have continued after the summer and to have grown and developed into a serious romance which would have led ultimately to marriage. The daily meetings, her whole relationship with him, had become during those weeks her sole reason for living. Other people had ceased to be important to her, but she had never asked him if he had had relatives and he had never told her about them or about his plans for the future.

That was why she had been so upset when he had left Balmore suddenly without telling her he would be leaving. Even now she could remember the hollow feeling of desolation she had experienced the day she had found the cottage door locked and his car gone. Thinking that he had gone only to Balvaig, she had lingered about the cottage for a long time, leaving only when hunger had driven her down the road towards the loch.

She had been halfway down the hillside when she had met Hamish Taggart on his way up. Lifting his cap to her, he had greeted her with his usual Highland courtesy, showing no surprise at meeting her there.

'Have you seen Neil Dysart?' she had asked, pushed into asking the question by the aching need to know that Neil would be returning soon.

'No. And I'm thinking we won't be seeing him here for a long time,' Hamish had replied.

'Oh. Why? Where has he gone?'

'Today he's away to Glasgow.'

'Well, that isn't far away, and I'll be going there myself in a few weeks' time,' she had replied, feeling hope surge back. Then remembering she had had no idea where Neil lived in the city she had asked, 'Do you know his address in Glasgow?'

'You could be asking Sir Alec,' Hamish had said in his vague way. 'Good evening to ye.' And he had lifted his cap and walked on up the hill.

It had taken Kirsty all next day to pluck up the courage to ask Alec about Neil, because she had been reluctant to admit to her employer that she had been meeting the doctor who had been holi-daying on one of the Balmore crofts, but even-tually she had found a way to ask him if he had known where Neil lived in Glasgow.

They had been sitting in Alec's study relaxing after working all afternoon on annotating the book he had written about the natural history of the Highlands. Alec had been sitting in his wheelchair behind the desk and he had given her a frowning glance.

'Why do you want to know where he lives?' he had asked.

'I'd like to get in touch with him when I go back there,' she had replied. Trying to appear casual, she had shuffled papers together pretending to tidy the desk.

'He doesn't live in Glasgow,' Alec had replied.

'But Hamish told me Neil went there yesterday,' she had retorted, looking across the desk at him. He had been looking at her an expression of sadness in his pale blue eyes.

'He went to Glasgow to catch a plane to London and from London he flew to the United States today.' Alec had looked at his wrist watch. 'He'll be in New York now,' he had added. 'He's going to work in a clinic there with a famous orthopaedic surgeon, and I doubt if he'll come back to this country once he's established as a surgeon over there. They make a lot of money, you know, in the States.'

Kirsty remembered feeling as if all the life had drained out of her. Her legs had shaken and she had sat down suddenly on the nearest chair. Her face had felt dry and taut and her eyes had burned.

Vaguely she had been aware of the swishing sound of the wheels of Alec's chair as it had skimmed over the floor and around the side of the desk towards her.

'Kirsty, what is it? What's wrong?' he had asked in a concerned voice.

Pride had come to her aid. Blinking back tears, she had forced her lips to smile and had said jauntily.

'Nothing.'

'Come now, my dear. *You* know that isn't true, and *I* know that you've been seeing Neil Dysart every day for the past four weeks.' Alec's voice had held a note of mockery.

'How do you know?' she had exclaimed. With his silvery fair hair, his almost round face and his blue eyes, he had always seemed to her to have been a middle-aged cherub, kind, gentle, helpful and understanding, but at that moment there had been something sinister in the way the pale eyes had stared at her.

'Even though I can't get about easily I know everything that goes on on the estate,' he had said softly.

'Did Hamish tell you?' she had asked.

'Hamish tells me only what he feels like telling me, unfortunately,' he had snapped, his lips thinning. 'But I know you've been visiting Neil Dysart because I've watched you walking in that direction every afternoon. I've seen you climb the hill and I've seen you go into the cottage. You've always stayed there a long time, all evening and sometimes all night.'

Her cheeks burning, she had stared at him, feeling the hairs prick at the back of her neck as for a moment she had had the wild fantastic idea that he had possessed occult powers. Then she had looked beyond him at the telescope on its tripod in the big window behind the desk. The window had a view of the loch and the heather-covered moors of Cairn Rua.

'You've been spying on me!' she had cried accusingly, and had sprung to her feet, revolted by the idea of him watching her through his spy-glass.

'Not spying, my dear. No, not spying. Just keeping watch over you,' he had replied, his face softening into an affectionate smile. 'You see, having brought you here to work for me I feel responsible for your welfare.' He had sighed heavily and had frowned as he had also looked at the telescope. Then he had shaken his head. 'Several times I've thought of warning you and then I've decided that you wouldn't listen to an old fuddy-duddy like me, that you'd think I was making a fuss about nothing.' He had looked at her again and had smiled. 'Young women are so sensible these days, and not easily fooled.'

'Warn me about what?' she had asked, sinking down on the chair.

'About Neil.' He had sighed again. 'He's a handsome lad, clever too, and very ambitious. I promised his father I'd keep an eye on him, see that he had a good education and followed a career. He's done well and now he has a chance to do better, and I don't blame him for taking that chance. In fact I've encouraged him to take it.' He had frowned down at his hands which were playing with a paper knife. 'I'm not sure of the best way of putting this,' he had continued. 'I've known Neil a long time and he's ... well, he's like his father, and where young women like yourself are concerned his morals are not of the best. He likes to ...' He had broken off, looking rather embarrassed.

'Play around?' Kirsty had suggested in a cool voice.

'You put it very well,' he had said, nodding his head.

'Oh, I knew he's like that.' Now, she didn't know how she had managed to sound so careless.

'Did you?' Alex had looked up in surprise. 'Oh, then that's a relief. I was afraid, you see, that you'd be hurt by his abrupt departure.'

'I am a little,' she had confessed. 'I mean, we've been quite friendly and you'd have thought, wouldn't you, that he'd have said something about going away.' She had stood up again and had begun to collect more papers together. 'But I'm not going to fall into a depression about it,' she had added with a lightness she had not been feeling. 'He's gone, and his way of going tells me that he feels about our brief friendship the same way I feel about it.'

'And how do you feel about it?' Alec had asked, looking at her curiously.

'It was fun while it lasted,' she had replied with a shrug and an impish smile. 'But I'm really glad it's over. Now I can concentrate better on helping you to finish the footnotes for this book before I go back to university.'

She had really meant what she had said to Alec that day, Kirsty thought now as she approached the stand of tiny trees, dark green feathery pines alternating with the slender silvery trunks of young birches. She had really believed that by saying she had been glad Neil had gone away and their affair had ended she would feel glad.

But it hadn't worked out that way. The wound he had inflicted had gone very deep, and in spite of being a sensible, practical young woman, not easily fooled, she had yearned desperately for Neil, hoping that he would write to her explaining why he had left so suddenly. She had hoped he would write to tell her he missed her, that he loved her and would be returning soon to Scotland to ask her to marry him. She had hoped he would write and ask her to fly out to New York and join him there after she had graduated.

A month after he had left Balmore she had left too, after promising Alec she would return the following summer to work for him on the estate. No letter had come from Neil and none arrived in the following months, and after a while Kirsty had accepted the fact that her first love affair was over.

With acceptance came a certain cynicism about young men. She had vowed secretly that she would never believe anything a man said to her. Never again would she let a man make love to her without making some sort of commitment to her and to her alone. Applying herself wholeheartedly to her studies, she had managed to achieve a brilliant degree and after she had graduated she had returned to Balmore. Alec had generously offered her the position of factor of the estate, an unusual appointment, because rarely had women been land stewards. Not long after she had taken the job he had told her one day, quite casually, that he had heard of Neil's marriage in the United States to Barbara Gow, heiress to the Gow millions. Six months later Alec had asked her to marry him, and the ceremony had taken place quietly in the old stone church at Balvaig.

CHAPTER THREE

AN hour after leaving the Lodge Kirsty emerged from the stand of new trees to find herself half way up Cairn Rua. She felt hot and her brow was beaded with drops of sweat. Pulling her sweater off, she tied the sleeves around her waist and flipped undone another button of her shirt. Far below her the loch was as still as a puddle caught in a rut and its earlier brilliance was dimmed by a heat haze. Behind her bees hummed ecstatically in the bell heather which had just bloomed in splashes of purple all over the moors. She glanced upwards. From among its sheltering drystone walls and tangled bushes Neil's cottage glinted at her.

Now she was so near she might as well go to see if he was there and deliver Hussein's invitation to tea, she thought, and she began to follow a narrow sheep path which twisted through the rough brown bushes of real heather which was not yet in flower. The path was steep and she walked slowly, feeling the sun's heat beating down on the back of her head and filtering through the thin stuff of her shirt.

When she reached the green level grass in front of the cottage she stopped to get her breath. Before the open door of the house Neil was sitting in an old deck chair, one leg bent, its foot resting on the knee of his other leg. Against the frame made by his bent leg he had rested a pad of paper and seemed to be drawing or writing on it.

Standing and staring, Kirsty had an uncanny feeling that four years hadn't gone by and that this was the day after the day when she had found the cottage locked and his car gone. The feeling was so strong that it pushed her forward through the opening in the low grey drystone wall which surrounded the cottage garden and along the path towards him.

The words 'Where were you yesterday?' were on the tip of her tongue and she was about to say them when he looked up, probably having heard her footsteps, and he wasn't the young man she had known, with mischief dancing in his clear amber eyes and laughter curving his lips. He was an older man; older, tougher and as wary as a wildcat, his eyes narrowing between dark lashes when he saw her and his lips curving sardonically.

She pulled up short bit back the words she had been going to say, schooled her face to smoothness and thrust her hands into the pockets of her pants.

'Good morning, Neil,' she said calmly.

His glance lifted to the sun, then returned to her face.

'It's just about afternoon,' he said. 'I wondered how long it would be before you came.' He tossed aside the pad of paper and rose to his feet.

'You can be sure I wouldn't have come if I hadn't a good reason,' she replied sharply, thinking he was implying that she couldn't stay away now that she knew he was at the cottage. 'I've come with an invitation. Hussein al Dukar would like you to have tea with him at the Lodge tomorrow afternoon.'

'Just me?' His eyebrows lifted in surprise.

'No. He's invited everyone who lives or works on the estate.'

'Why?'

'Because he wants to meet everyone, of course.'

'Is this your idea?'

'No. His own. He wants to find out who helped the two young men who were caught poaching yesterday to escape.'

'Really?' This time the tilt to his eyebrows was mocking. 'Doesn't he know? Haven't you told him?'

'How could I tell him? I didn't see who it was.'

'And that's your only reason for coming all this way, to issue an invitation from him?' he queried.

'Yes,' she snapped, suddenly irritated by his mockery.

'You could have sent Hamish,' he suggested.

'I could, but I happened to be over this side of the loch inspecting the new plantation of trees on the lower slopes. You must have noticed them.'

'I have. They're growing well.' His glance drifted over her and again she sensed he was laughing at her. 'I guess you're good at your job and Alec made a good choice when he hired you to be factor,' he added.

They stood facing each other in the same way they had stood the day before on the road to the Lodge, and again Kirsty had the impression that they were enemies more than they were friends.

She searched her mind for something to say, anything to bridge the sudden awkward silence.

'My brother asked me to tell you that he saw your friends in their car going towards Fort William when he was returning to Balvaig yesterday afternoon,' she said. 'He'd noticed the Rolls coming this way and so he drove in the opposite direction with the security guards Hussein sent after you, to give your friends time to collect their gear and make a getaway.'

'That was helpful of him. Please thank him for the lads and for me when you see him again,' he replied coolly.

'I asked him to go with the security guards when Hussein ordered them to chase the Rolls,' she added.

'Then my thanks to you too,' he said, his eyebrows lifting again in surprise. 'I had a feeling you would disapprove of what I did. And that's why I thought you'd come here today, to give me a piece of your mind.' The glint in his eyes challenged her.

'Well, I have to admit I wasn't exactly pleased by what you did,' Kirsty retorted spiritedly. 'Hussein was very upset when he found his car had been taken. Why couldn't you have taken mine, or even Duncan's?'

'Because the Sheikh's was there in the garage when we climbed down from the hayloft and the keys were in it. It was just asking to be taken. And also I guessed it would hurt him if his expensive status symbol went missing for a few hours.'

'But you didn't have to rescue them,' she argued. 'I could have talked Hussein into letting them go, I know I could—I'd already persuaded him not to send for the police because there was no evidence that they were the poachers. They didn't have a fish or a weapon when they were caught.'

'How was I to know whose side you were on?' he asked. 'As factor you had every right to call in the police and I had to get my friends away from here before you did, so I acted accordingly. You see, my friends were unknown to Hamish or to anyone else on the estate and as long as they remained unknown there was a chance for them. I didn't want the affair investigated by the police or their names would have appeared in the local papers. They're both training to be surgeons, so their professional reputations had to be protected. That more than anything else moved me to do what I did.' He paused and devilry glinted again in his eyes. 'Although I also wanted to teach the Sheikh a lesson and to show him he can't play the tyrant here like he can in his own country.'

'Hussein wasn't playing the tyrant,' she retorted hotly. 'He's ignorant of the way the law works in this country, that's all, and he hasn't been here long enough to understand some of our customs. But at least he's showing he's willing to learn by inviting everyone to tea. Will you come tomorrow?'

'Will you be there?'

'Of course.'

'Then I might come.'

Another silence. She supposed Neil was waiting for her to leave, since he hadn't invited her to sit down and hadn't offered her any hospitality. But now that she was there it seemed wrong to leave and much more natural to stay, to linger in the flower-scented, bee-loud garden with him as she had often lingered four years ago, to talk lazily of this and that and eventually . . . to make love.

Kirsty glanced away from him quickly, down at the sketchbook on the grass.

'I see you still draw,' she murmured.

'I haven't done any sketching since I was last here,' he replied. 'I've almost forgotten how.' He shrugged indifferently.

'I wondered . . . I mean, Duncan suggested that you might like to have the two watercolours your mother painted and gave to your father.' She saw him stiffen and added hurriedly, 'Neil, why didn't you tell me you're Ian Whyte's younger son?'

'I've told you why I didn't. I thought you knew, that Alec had told you.'

'You should have told me yourself,' she insisted.

'It wasn't important at the time.' He looked right into her eyes. 'You and I had other things on our minds, if you care to remember,' he added softly.

To her surprise her heart leapt with sudden joy because after all he had remembered too that time of loving companionship they had known. The heat of passion pulsed through her unexpectedly as if she had been in his arms, moulded against his lean muscular body, lying among the heather on a hot August afternoon, his lips searing her throat, his hands sliding over her from shoulder to thigh.

'I remember,' she whispered shakily. 'But I thought you'd forgotten. You left so suddenly, without a word, and you didn't write to me.'

He stepped back from her, his eyes narrowing warily, his eyebrows slanting in a frown.

'There didn't seem much point in writing to a two-timing cheat who hadn't meant a word she'd said and who'd only been interested in having a sexual fling with me while she made up to her employer, a man with a title and an estate,' he retorted, his lips thinning to a cruel taut line.

Kirsty saw red. Her arm swung up and the flat of her hand struck his face. The loud sound of the slap brought her to her senses. She stepped back and stared at the red marks left by her fingers appearing on his tanned cheek.

'Feel better now?' Neil asked tauntingly.

'You deserved it,' she retorted breathlessly.

'For telling the truth?' he jeered.

'For calling me a cheat!' she flared, anger boiling up within her again as she recalled how unhappy she had been after he had left four years ago, the long dreary months of hoping and waiting for a letter from him; the cold raw ache of disillusionment when no letter had come. 'I wasn't the cheat—you were. You were the one who didn't mean what you said, and you were too much of a coward to tell me you didn't want me any more, so you left.' Her breath hissed as she drew it in sharply. Now she was angry with herself for letting him see how much he had hurt her. With a great effort she controlled her feelings and glanced deliberately at her watch. 'I must get back to the Lodge,' she said as coolly as she could, 'I haven't time to stay and rake over dead ashes with you.'

'No one was asking you to,' he retorted nastily. 'I didn't ask you to come here today.'

It was the last straw. Turning on her heel, Kirsty didn't run away, she marched, her head held high. Right through the opening of the gate she went and turned left to take the rough road which slanted down to the lochside road. It was a good thing she knew the way without looking, she thought with self-mockery, because she was so angry she could hardly see.

By the time she reached the other road she was feeling more calm, but she was wishing she hadn't gone to see Neil. She had been foolish to let herself be tempted into going to his cottage, into hoping that they could at least be friends again even if they couldn't be lovers. Cautiously she glanced back over her shoulder to see if he had followed her as he had followed her the day before. But he hadn't. And why should he? One way and another he had made it very clear that he didn't like her.

But where had he got the idea that she had been cheating four years ago? As she walked along Kirsty frowned at the spurts of pale dust churned up by her leather brogues. Who had suggested to him that she had been making up to Alec at the same time she had been visiting him at his cottage? Who, apart from Hamish, had known she had been friendly with Neil? Only Alec, and he had warned her against him. Oh, Neil must have invented the whole story to excuse his own cowardly behaviour.

Tossing back her head, she strode along, pretending she didn't care that Neil believed she had been two-timing him four years ago. What did it matter now anyway? He was married and he probably had a son or a daughter by now, perhaps both. She frowned again. She didn't really know if he had a family or not, because after informing her that Neil had married Barbara Gow Alec had never mentioned him again. Nor had she.

There was a lot Alec hadn't told her. He'd been a very secretive man. For instance, he hadn't told her that Balmore was mortgaged to the hilt. He had taken out the mortgage apparently when he had begun to employ her as factor. He had done it to finance the re-afforestation of the estate and to renovate the house.

Balmore had been his obsession, and everything and everyone had been subservient to that obsession. He had only asked her to marry him because he had known she could run the estate exactly as he had wanted it run but had been too incapable of doing as the dreaded multiple sclerosis had eventually overwhelmed him. And she had married him, as Neil had suggested yesterday, because she had been sorry for him and had wanted to help him. She had never thought for a moment that he had intended to leave Balmore to her in his will.

In leaving the estate to her had he really bypassed Neil, to whom it should have been left? And why hadn't Alec told her Neil was his half-brother? Perhaps he had thought she had known. Or perhaps he had thought she would guess there was some relationship between him and Neil when he had told her he had promised Neil's father he would keep an eye on him.

'He's like his father,' Alec had said. Had that been a hint? If it had she hadn't taken it, because she hadn't known what Sir Ian Whyte had looked like. His portrait didn't hang in the gallery with the portraits of the other Whyte baronets and there had been no photographs of him about the house. And since there had been no resemblance whatsoever between Alec and Neil she couldn't have possibly guessed that they had been fathered by the same man.

As soon as she could she was going to the room in the turret to look at the portrait Duncan had mentioned. Kirsty put on speed and almost ran along the road to the Lodge. After a quick lunch in the factor's house she sat down at her desk to open letters and to answer some of them. Once the correspondence was done she went over to the Lodge to find Mary Taggart.

'I'd like to have a look at the upstairs room in the turret,' she said to the housekeeper. 'My brother said you told him there were some paintings up there. I'd like to see them.'

'Ach, have ye never been up there?' exclaimed Mary, her reddish-brown eyes rolling expressively.

'No, I haven't. Sir Alec said it was just full of old junk.'

'Now, fancy him saying a thing like that,' remarked Mary. 'It was his father's favourite room, so it was. Sir Ian had his bed there and all his favourite paintings. Come along then and I'll be showing it to you myself. Perhaps ye'd like to be opening it up and having it used now that Sir Alec has gone?'

The turret was really a separate building from the Lodge and was all that remained of an old castle which had once been situated on the green hill which commanded a view of Glen Lannach. There were two entrances, one from the courtyard and another from the kitchen which had been put in during Sir Ian's time, Mary explained, so that he could go to his room without going outside the house.

'There are only two rooms in the tower,' said Mary breathlessly as they walked up the circular flight of stairs set into the thickness of the walls of the turret. 'You can only get into the lower room from the outside, and that's the one that's full of old furniture and junk. Sir Ian once told me it was the place where the servants would live and cook, and the room upstairs would be where the clan chieftain and his lady and their children would sleep. Ach, it must have been very over-crowded to my way of thinking, as well as un-sanitary, and I'm glad I didn't live in those times.'

'I hadn't realised before that you knew Sir Ian,' said Kirsty as she followed Mary up the next

spiral of stairs. Sunlight shafting in through the
narrow slits of windows struck diamond sparks
from the rough stone from which the tower had
been built.

'It was Sir Ian himself that asked me to be
housekeeper, soon after his wife died, Lady
Constance, that was,' replied Mary.

'What was Sir Ian like?'

'He was a fine man, handsome and generous,
some might call him extravagant. He was a surgeon and spent most of his time in Edinburgh
and only came to Balmore for his holidays. Aye,'
sighed Mary, 'it was a sad blow to him when his
wife died before she could have any more children. He loved her dearly and never married
again.' Mary stopped outside a stout oak door set
into the curving inside wall and inserted a key in
the lock. 'Not that he didn't have a few affairs
after Lady Constance died, if ye ken my meaning,'
she added with a sly wink. She opened the door
and pushed it wide. 'So here ye are. Step inside
and see for yerself if I'm not telling the truth when
I say Sir Ian was handsome.'

The room was, of course, round, and surpris-
ingly light, having a wide curved window which
looked out over the loch towards Cairn Rua. It
was furnished not with junk but with a wide comfortable bed covered with a brocade cover, a big
wardrobe, a chest of drawers and a dressing table
and two armchairs. The floor was completely
covered with a thick blue and pink Chinese carpet.
Against the end of the bed a large painting in a
gilt frame, like the frames surrounding the por-

traits in the gallery, was resting, put there presumably by Duncan.

Standing in front of the portrait, Kirsty stared at it in amazement. Only a few hours ago she had stood and stared at a man who had looked very like the man in the portrait. The hair was a different colour, it was true. Ian Whyte's hair had been dark brown, not chestnut, but the deep peak was there, the haughty arching eyebrows were the same and the clear amber eyes seemed to glance at her down the aquiline nose in the same way Neil had glanced at her so many times. Perhaps the mouth and chin were different, Neil's mouth being wider and his chin more angular than those of the man in the portrait, but any stranger knowing one of them and then seeing the other would know at once they were related. Of Alec there was nothing in the painted face.

'Sir Alec must have looked more like his mother,' Kirsty murmured.

'Well now, I'm not so sure. Lady Constance was a small thing, black-haired and blue-eyed. She was a dainty wee thing and not given to childbearing, I'm thinking. Sir Alec now was always fair-haired and big-boned.'

'Do you know why this portrait is here and not in the gallery?' asked Kirsty, walking over to the window and looking across the loch to Cairn Rua. The weather was changing. Heat had caused big clouds to build up and the sky was no longer blue but had taken on a yellowish tinge. The water of the loch was a sullen grey and even as she looked out she heard the distant growl of thunder and a few raindrops spattered against the windowpane.

'Sir Alec had it put up here when the gallery was redecorated,' replied Mary. 'Everything else belonging to his father was up here, so I suppose he thought the portrait should be here too.'

Or he didn't want anyone to see how like Sir Ian the son of Morag Dysart looked, thought Kirsty with a sudden flash of insight into the workings of Alec's mind. He hadn't wanted her to come up here in case she had seen the portrait. He hadn't wanted her to know that Neil was his half-brother. Why?

'And these are the paintings I was telling your brother about,' Mary was saying as Kirsty swung away from the window to look round. The paintings were small, about eighteen inches by fourteen inches, framed simply and covered with glass. They were exquisite delicate colour washes of the view across the loch from the high turret room and of the view from the cottage on Cairn Rua of the loch and the tower. Lifting them off the wall, Kirsty examined the backs of them. The dedication was written on the back as Duncan had described. She looked at Mary Taggart.

'Morag Dysart was Sir Ian's mistress. wasn't she?' she said.

'Aye, aye, just so, just so,' sighed Mary, nodding her head. 'He gave her yon croft to live in when he knew she was expecting his child. She stayed there until he died and then she went away to Edinburgh to be near the boy while he was at school there. She died just over four years ago.'

Four years ago Neil had come to stay at the croft which he had inherited from his mother.

'I didn't know. Oh, Mary, I didn't know about her and Sir Ian. No one told me,' she muttered, and laid the picture down on the top of the chest of drawers. 'Sir Alec never told me he had a half-brother. Do you know why he didn't tell me?'

'If you want my honest opinion,' said Mary in her blunt matter of fact way, 'I think Sir Alec was jealous of Neil Dysart. And why shouldn't he be? Neil had everything Sir Alec didn't have. Neil was strong and clever, not pulled down by that awful creeping paralysis. Neil was handsome and popular with women, and most of all he was the constant reminder of Sir Ian's close association with Morag Dysart, the young woman Sir Alec had always fancied for himself.'

Kirsty looked up sharply from the paintings to stare at the housekeeper.

'Mary, you're not saying that Sir Alec and Morag Dysart were once lovers?' she gasped.

'No, I'm not saying that. I don't think she gave Sir Alec another thought once she had met his father. But it was Sir Alec who introduced her to Sir Ian when he brought her here one summer. That would be when he was about nineteen, just before the paralysis began to show itself. He met her in Edinburgh when he was studying at the university there. She was three or four years older than he was, tall with long red-gold hair and dark brown eyes, a lovely-looking lass, but a wee bit strange and wild, ye ken.'

'My brother says she was a very good artist, and her paintings are worth a lot of money now.'

'Then you could be selling those two and some of the others and paying off those debts instead of letting the place to yon Sheikh,' said Mary tartly. 'Ach, that Arab cook and those bodyguards are enough to drive me out of my mind! They're for-ever watching everything I do. As if I'd be want-ing to poison him.' Mary folded her arms across her ample bosom and glared at Kirsty. 'I may as well be telling you while I've got you to myself for a few minutes, this letting of the estate to foreigners with outlandish names and queer customs isn't at all popular with the people on the estate or in the village.'

'So I've gathered,' replied Kirsty, stiffening up. 'But perhaps I'm not popular either because I've inherited the estate; because I'm not the natural heir.'

'Aye, you could say that,' said Mary with brutal frankness. 'And if you really belonged to the Highlands you would never have considered let-ting the place to an outsider.'

'I suppose everyone had known except me that Neil Dysart is the natural heir to Balmore,' Kirsty muttered miserably.

'Not everyone, but most of the older folk know,' said Mary, her reddish-brown eyes hard and hos-tile. 'What are you going to do about it now that you know?'

'I don't know. I . . . I'm not sure that there is anything I can do,' replied Kirsty, wishing now that she hadn't said anything to Mary. Finding out the truth had made her feel suddenly very insecure and she had a strong desire to turn and run far away from Balmore and its responsibilities. She wanted to be Kirsty Ure again, young and free, single and lighthearted, not Christina, Lady Whyte, widowed and bowed down with the burden of debts her late husband had left to her.

'Have ye seen all ye want to see now?' asked Mary.

'Yes, thanks. But I'd like the portrait taken down to the gallery and hung there . . . over the hearth . . . before the tea party tomorrow. From the look of the weather now we'd better be prepared to serve tea in the gallery. I wouldn't be at all surprised if it doesn't rain for a few days now that it's started.'

Her prediction was right. Next morning was grey and wet and the rain continued into the afternoon so the tea-party could not be held on the terrace as Hussein had hoped. He was very disappointed, but cheered up when Kirsty told him tea would be served in the long gallery instead.

A fire was lit in the great stone hearth and a long refectory table, covered with a white cloth, was set with plates of tiny sandwiches, cream cakes and biscuits, all made by Mary Taggart who presided over the tea urn and the cups and saucers. The flickering firelight, the soft rosy glow from various table and standard lamps did much to create a warm almost festive atmosphere, setting at bay the grey gloom of the day outdoors.

From their portraits the Whyte baronets of the past looked down their aquiline noses in haughty surprise at the gathering.

As Kirsty had guessed, everyone who lived or worked on the estate and even a few villagers came to tea to meet Hussein out of sheer curiosity, and from three o'clock onwards she was busy at the top of the stairs greeting and introducing farmers, crofters, gamekeepers, gardeners and foresters and their wives to the Sheikh. Soon the gallery was echoing to the sing-song hum of many Highland voices and the tinkle of china cups against china saucers.

She was talking to Monsieur and Madame Delacroix and watching how Camille was never far away from Hussein as he chatted with perfect courtesy and amiability to one of the gardeners when Neil walked into the gallery.

Looking every inch the successful doctor and surgeon in a well-tailored suit of fine greenish tweed, his chestnut-coloured hair smoothly brushed and shining with reddish lights, he paused at the top of the staircase to look round and the aquiline cast of his features, the straight proud set of his shoulders, the cool amber glance of his eyes were so like those of the man in the portrait which hung over the hearth that Kirsty was sure most people in the gallery would notice the strong family resemblance and comment on it.

His glance alighted on her and he moved towards her. Excusing herself to Monsieur and Madame Delacroix, she walked across to meet

him, aware that her colour had heightened and
that her heart had begun to pound excitedly.

'I was beginning to think you wouldn't come,'
she murmured when she was close to him.

He gave her a mocking glance and held out his
right hand. For the sake of appearances Kirsty
put her right hand in his. At once he raised her
hand and bending his head brushed the back of
her hand with his lips. At their touch hot colour
ran up into her cheeks and it took all her self-
control to stop herself from snatching her hand
from his grasp.

'Did you have to do that?' she whispered
through tautly smiling lips.

'I always like to show my appreciation of feminine beauty, and you're looking remarkably
elegant this afternoon, Lady Whyte. This is, I believe, the first time I've ever seen you in a dress.'
His eyes gleaming with wickedly blatant admiration he looked her up and down insolently. 'And
you should wear blue more often. It enhances the
colour of your eyes.' He paused, then added with
a sardonic grin, 'Are you still angry with me?'

'Was I angry?' she retorted, arching her eyebrows at him in mock surprise.

'If you weren't you gave a good impression of
being angry yesterday, and my cheek still stings.'
He fingered his left cheek. 'I've only come this
afternoon to seek my revenge.' He leaned forward
suddenly and whispered right into her ear so that
his breath tickled the skin, 'No woman, not even
you, my dear, slaps my face, calls me a coward
and gets away with it!'

Her cheeks now blazing red, Kirsty stepped back quickly glancing sideways hoping that no one had noticed how closely he had approached her and finding, to her chagrin, that several people were watching them, including Camille who, for once, wasn't with Hussein, but was with her mother, and who began to sidle back to Hussein to draw his attention to Neil.

'I'll fetch you a cup of tea,' Kirsty muttered to Neil, and would have stepped away from him, but he caught hold of her arm and said,

'Whose portrait is hanging over the hearth?'

She gave him a surprised glance. He was staring at the painting in puzzlement.

'Don't you recognise him?' she said. 'He's Sir Ian Whyte. That's the portrait Duncan found in the turret room——' She broke off, aware that Hussein and Camille were approaching.

'I do not think we have met,' said Hussein politely. Beside Neil he looked slight, very dark and, for once, very boyish. 'I am Hussein al Dukar.'

'Neil Dysart,' replied Neil, shaking hands. 'I'm the tenant of the croft on Cairn Rua.'

'Forgive me for being personal,' said Hussein charmingly, 'but you do not seem to be like the other crofters here.'

'Neil is a surgeon,' said Kirsty quickly. 'He comes to the croft only for holidays.'

'Aren't you going to introduce me?' Camille said, in her attractively deep husky voice, and reminded of his duty, Hussein turned to her quickly.

'*Excusez-moi, mon amie,*' he murmured. 'Mr Dysart, this is Mademoiselle Camille Delacroix, a friend of mine from Paris.'

Camille was looking very lovely and chic, Kirsty thought, in a dress of brilliant emerald green silk with a plain tunic-type top fitted over a knife-pleated skirt. Neil greeted her in French with a suave gallantry which Kirsty realised he must have inherited from his father and Camille responded charmingly, showing more animation in her face than she had all the time she had been at Balmore.

'I cannot 'elp but notice, Monsieur Dysart,' the French girl said, 'that you are very like the man in the portrait which 'angs over the 'earth. You are related perhaps to the family which own this *château*?'

Above Camille's shining blonde head Neil sent Kirsty a murderous glance. Returning it with a mocking smile and a nod, she excused herself to Hussein, having noticed that Ahmed, the big bodyguard, was coming across the gallery, his sharp black eyes fixed on Neil. As she walked over to the table to talk to Mary Taggart Kirsty couldn't help laughing to herself. Not only would Neil have to explain his likeness to the portrait over the hearth, he would very soon have to answer Ahmed's charges that he was the person who had helped the poachers to escape the previous day.

Standing behind the table with Mary, she served tea and talked with various people, occasionally sparing a glance at the group of four standing near the hearth, half expecting to see Ahmed seize hold of Neil and march him out of the room to lock him up somewhere. She could see that Neil was talking and that both Camille and Hussein seemed to be entranced by what he was saying to them. Particularly did Camille seem to be entranced, thought Kirsty waspishly, and suddenly she saw Neil through the eyes of the eighteen-year-old French girl.

He was the handsome older man, impeccably dressed, with the aura of success glowing about him, experienced with just a touch of cynicism in his attractively tanned lean face to hint at a mysterious and possibly outrageous past, sexually magnetic to a woman of Camille's tender age . . .

No, no! Kirsty found herself wanting to rush across the room to Camille and to warn her against Neil, but at that moment he stopped speaking and Ahmed stepped forward to say something. Camille and Hussein both burst out laughing. Ahmed looked embarrassed and Neil looked wickedly amused. Hussein placed a hand on the arm of his bodyguard and turned Ahmed away from Neil and Camille to speak to him confidentially. Left to themselves, Camille and Neil chatted for a few moments, then linking her arm through one of Neil's Camille guided him towards her parents, presumably to introduce him to them.

'No!' said Kirsty loudly and vehemently, and actually stamped her foot on the floor.

'Is it to yourself you're after talking or to me?' asked Mary Taggart amiably.

'To myself,' muttered Kirsty, glancing across to the Delacroix family again. Camille and her parents and Neil were leaving the gallery by way of the stairs and again she felt she wanted to run after them, to butt in on their conversation, to insert herself somehow between Camille and Neil.

'Everyone seems to be leaving now and the Sheikh is saying goodbye,' Mary said, 'so I'm thinking we could be collecting up the cups and saucers and taking them back to the kitchen. Ye'll no mind helping me?'

'No, not at all,' sighed Kirsty.

An hour later, when she was thinking of leaving the kitchen after having helped Mary to wash up and put everything away, Neil walked into the room. Mary greeted him cheerfully and with obvious affection.

'Ach, it's grand to be seeing ye again, so it is. Hamish was telling me ye're staying at Cairn Rua. Ye'll be seeing a lot of changes in the glen, I've no doubt.' Mary sent a sly glance in Kirsty's direction. 'Lady Whyte here is responsible for many of them. There isn't anything she doesn't know about planting forests and looking after the land. Was there something you were wanting, now?'

'A few words with Lady Whyte, that's all,' said Neil coolly.

'Then I'll be away to my own house now before that Arab cook starts making a mess of my kitchen,' said Mary. 'I'll be seeing you tomorrow, my lady,' she added, putting on her tough

Burberry raincoat and slipping her feet into wellington boots. 'Good day to both of you.'

She left the room, and Kirsty began to take off the apron she had worn to help with the washing up.

'Why did you hang my father's portrait in the gallery?' demanded Neil.

'I decided it should be restored to its proper place,' she replied. 'I was surprised you didn't recognise him.'

'How could I recognise him? As far as I know I never saw him when he was alive.'

'But surely he visited you and your mother when you lived at the croft.'

'Possibly he did visit my mother, but not when I was capable of remembering him or when I was present.' His mouth twisted. 'I didn't even know he was my father until my mother told me, four years ago just before she died. I came back here then to stay at the croft and to see Alec.' He gave a short mirthless laugh. 'He was furious with me for turning up, and now I've seen that portrait I can understand why. He didn't like having his father's bastard staying here. Did you see the other paintings when you were in the turret room, the ones painted by my mother?'

'Yes, I did.'

'I'd like to see them, and I'd also like to accept your offer of them. Is the turret open?'

'No. But the key to the room is here.' Kirsty went over to the wall board where all the keys for various parts of the house were hung and took out the bunch of three large keys for the turret

doors. Turning round, she offered them to Neil.
He looked down at them, then slowly took the
keys from her hand. 'The door to the turret is
over there,' she added, pointing. 'And when
you've finished up there please lock both doors
again and put the keys back on the board.'

'I'd like you to come with me, Kirsty,' he said,
stepping in front of her as she started to leave the
kitchen.

'I really don't have the time. Excuse me,' she
replied briskly. She made to step around him, but
he sidestepped in front of her.

'No, I won't excuse you,' he said. 'As the lady
of the house you should be there when I take the
paintings, a witness to the event.'

She stared up at him searchingly, trying to
guess what was behind his request. The amber-
brown eyes looked back at her coolly, not a flicker
of mockery in them.

'Oh, all right, I'll come,' she sighed. 'This way.'

He unlocked the door, but she led the way
through and up the winding stairway. Compared
with the day before the light slanting through the
slit windows was full and they seemed to go
upwards through a grey mistiness as if they were
moving in a dream. The round upstairs room was
also full of misty grey light and the view from the
window of the loch and Cairn Rua had almost
disappeared behind a curtain of drizzling rain.

Kirsty snapped a switch and two lamps came
on. The blue and pink carpet glowed softly and
the brocade bedcover glinted with gold threads.
Neil closed the door. The key clocked in the lock

and Kirsty turned quickly from the window in time to see him put the bunch of keys in his jacket pocket.

He leaned against the door in the shadow cast by the bedside lamps and there was something vaguely menacing about his casual stance that tripped her nerves, causing them to tingle with apprehension.

'Why have you locked the door?' she demanded, going across the room towards him.

'To keep you in here and other people out,' he replied softly, stepping towards her. They met at the end of the bed. His eyes glowed yellow like a cat's in the dark as they looked right into hers and there was savagery in the sensual curl of his slightly parted lips. 'It's time you and I had a heart-to-heart talk, in private, Lady Whyte,' he murmured. 'And I think this is as good a way as any to begin.'

Kirsty stepped back too late. His hands gripped her shoulders mercilessly. She was jerked forward. Her head swung back and as she opened her mouth to protest against the pain which shot through her neck his mouth came down to cover hers in a hot hungry kiss.

She could have resisted. She could have hit at him with her fists and kicked him in the shins with the pointed toes of her shoes. But she did neither, because at the touch of his lips against hers all the hungry physical yearnings she had been suppressing over the past few years exploded upwards, shattering her defences against invasion.

Her arms went around his neck to hold him closer. Her body, taut and twanging with desire, pressed against his in shameless self-surrender. Being close to him was like arriving home after a long and lonely journey. It was like entering a warm and candlelit room after being outside in cold darkness, and when his arms closed strongly about her and he lifted her to carry her to the bed and lay her down upon it, it seemed to her the most natural thing for him to do.

Mouth to mouth, heart to heart, legs entwined, they lay while their fingers sought to undo buttons and fastenings and stroke away clothing. His kisses were like dark red wine going to her head and under her fingertips his warm skin was like velvet. She became almost delirious with sensuousness and moved against him provocatively and appealingly, knowing instinctively how to arouse and increase his desire yet uneasily aware that to give in to her desire to love him again might lead to some sort of disaster.

CHAPTER FOUR

ROUND and round, down and down, she seemed to be falling, spinning into the dark depths of sensuous pleasure where there was no coherent thought, only the tingle of titillation and the sweet joyous leap of passionate response, where there were no sounds save the thud of her excited heart in her ears and her sighing moans of entreaty.

Then suddenly Neil moved away from her, although his hands still clung to the soft curves of her breasts.

'Hell and damnation,' he whispered.

'What's the matter?' Kirsty asked, sitting up, the straps of her underslip sliding down her arms.

'I think I heard someone come into the tower,' he replied his hot glance arrowing in the direction of her half-exposed pink-tipped breasts. 'But I could have been mistaken.' With a hand on her shoulder he pulled her down against him again and dragged her head back so he could ravage her mouth in arrogant demand.

Her senses were beginning to reel again when someone turned the doorknob and tried to push the door open. Kirsty froze where she was, her whole body going stiff. Neil lifted his mouth from hers and grinned at her, his eyes glinting with unkind amusement.

'Are you afraid someone will come in and find

you in bed with one of your tenants, Lady *Chatterley* Whyte?' he scoffed. 'Don't worry—the door is locked. No one can come in.'

He had hardly finished speaking when the person outside the door thumped on it and rattled the doorknob.

'Who is in there? I can hear you speaking. Open the door at once or I will break it down!'

'It's Ahmed,' Kirsty gasped, sitting up again, and suddenly the whole door shook as the weight and strength of Ahmed's massive body was thrust against it.

'To hell with him,' growled Neil, and rolling off the bed he began to pull on his shirt. 'Who does he think he is, going round trying to break down doors?' Picking up his jacket, he took the bunch of keys from his pocket. Immediately Kirsty jumped off the bed and began to dress quickly.

'No, no,' she whispered desperately, 'don't open the door yet. Wait until I'm dressed.'

'Who is there?' shouted Ahmed, and thumped on the door again. 'Open the door!'

Neil thrust the tails of his shirt into the waist-band of his trousers, raked tousled hair back from his brow and advanced to the door. The lock clicked back and the door swung open just as Kirsty finished fastening the belt of her dress.

'Oh, it's you,' said Neil unpleasantly as he faced up to Ahmed. 'What do you want?'

Ahmed's black eyes widened in surprise. It seemed he had not expected to see Neil. Then he looked at Kirsty, who was standing at the end of the bed without shoes on her feet, her usually coiled-up hair hanging like a curtain of black silk about her face and shoulders.

'I am sorry, my lady,' Ahmed said stiffly. 'I see a light shining out from the tower window and I wonder who is in here.' His glance wandered from Kirsty, to the rumpled bed, and then down to the floor where Kirsty's dark filmy nylon tights lay close to her black shoes.

'Mr Dysart and I are just looking through the contents of this room,' Kirsty explained, drawing herself up to her full height and trying to look every inch the lady of the manor. 'Some of them belong to him and he is deciding what to take away with him. We won't be here much longer.'

Ahmed frowned uncertainly, then gave Neil a suspicious look.

'Well?' said Neil sharply. 'What are you waiting for? Didn't you hear what Lady Whyte said? We won't be here much longer. And we don't need a bodyguard watching over us.'

Ahmed hesitated for a few more seconds, his glance flitting from Neil back to Kirsty.

'You will be sure to lock the door to the tower, my lady,' he said. 'We cannot be too careful after what happened yesterday. We do not want any more strangers finding their way into the buildings.'

'I understand,' said Kirsty placatingly. 'And I'll be sure to lock up. Please go now.'

Ahmed inclined his head politely, gave Neil another suspicious glance and turning away went down the stairs. Neil shut the door and locked it again.

'Ahmed knows you helped the poachers to escape,' said Kirsty. She picked up her tights and leaning against the bed began to roll them on to her feet.

'I know he does,' said Neil. 'He told his lord and master he recognised me as the driver of the Rolls when we were all in the gallery.'

'So what did you say?'

'I didn't have to say anything. Camille Delacroix came to my rescue.'

'Oh. How?' Kirsty felt an unusual prick of jealousy at the mention of the young Frenchwoman's name.

'I'd just told her and Hussein that I'm the second son of Sir Ian Whyte and half-brother of your late husband. They were most impressed, and when Ahmed made his accusation they laughed at him and Camille said she couldn't possibly believe that I could have anything to do with poachers. Fortunately the Sheikh was more inclined to agree with her than with Ahmed.' He paused, then added roughly, '*God*, it infuriates me to see those security men snooping around Balmore! I wish now I'd locked the other door from the inside and then we wouldn't have been bothered by him.'

'Ahmed was only doing his job, making sure that Hussein is safe,' said Kirsty, slipping her feet into her shoes.

'Oh, sure,' Neil jeered. 'But I'm willing to bet he's gone now, hotfoot, to inform the Sheikh that you're not the prim and proper lady you seem to be.' He laughed and gave her a glance which was brimful of mockery as he approached her. 'He'd only have to take one look at you to guess what we've been doing.' Raising a hand, he pushed back a swathe of hair from her throat and his fingers lingered lightly but dangerously against her skin. 'You look as if you've been very thoroughly made love to, my raven-haired, blue-eyed lady,' he added softly, and bent his head to kiss her lips again.

'No!' Kirsty sprang away from him. 'Keep away from me! I'm not going to let you have your revenge.'

'Revenge? What revenge?'

'You said you'd only come today to get your revenge for what I said to you yesterday about being a coward, and I suppose that was what was going to happen there on the bed. You thought you'd punish me by taking me against my will.'

Neil stared at her for a moment in surprised silence. Then he began to laugh.

'So it was going to be against your will, was it?' he mocked. 'Somehow I don't think so. You were very willing, far more willing than I'd expected. In fact I got the impression that my kisses were most welcome and that you'd been longing to be made love to for a long time.' He stepped towards her again. 'Remember the first time we kissed, Kirsty?' he whispered, his eyes taking on that dark topaz glow. 'You looked so lovely and untouched as you sat in the old chair at the cottage that I couldn't believe you were real. I had to kiss you to find out if you were flesh and blood or merely someone I'd dreamed up, a fantasy lover. Your lips were as soft and delicate as thistledown and they didn't know how to kiss.' His mouth twisted cynically. 'But they soon learned. By God, how soon they learned!' His voice grated with bitterness. 'Yet still I believed you to be innocent.'

'I was!' she cried in outrage. 'You were the first one who'd kissed me like that.'

'I doubt it,' he sneered.

'Oh!' Furious with herself because she had been betrayed into telling him something she had had no intention of telling him, Kirsty swung away from him and collecting her long hair in one hand to hold it back at her nape she went over to the dressing table to look for something to tie her hair back with. 'Anyway,' she raged on, 'your kisses were suspect too. They had nothing to do with love, just as what you were doing a few minutes ago on that bed had nothing to do with love either, even though you call it "making love!"'

She opened the tiny drawers in the base of the old-fashioned mirror on the dressing table and to her surprise found it full of feminine knick-knacks, hairpins and slides, and some pieces of coloured ribbons. Taking a length of red ribbon, she tied her hair at the back of her neck. When it was done she turned to face Neil again.

'You don't know what love is. You wouldn't be here if you did,' she accused. 'You'd still be in New York with your wife.' She gave him a scornful glare. 'Oh, you haven't changed really. You still like to play around and to lead a woman on into believing you love her so you can take what you want from her. Well, this afternoon I was going to turn the tables on you if Ahmed hadn't interrupted us. I was going to lead you on and make you believe I was willing to make love, so that I could take what I wanted from you!'

His face went white under the summer tan and between their dark lashes his eyes glittered murderously. Muttering something virulent, he raked a hand through his hair and turned away. Going over to the window, he stood there looking out, his hands in his trouser pockets. After a while he said in a cold clipped voice,

'There's a good view of Cairn Rua from here, on a clear day, that is. Better than the view from the study where Alec used to work and where he had his telescope.' He looked over his shoulder at her. 'Did you know he used to watch you going over to the cottage?' he asked.

'Yes, he told me. But how do you know he used to watch me?'

'Because he told me too.' He paused, then added in a lower tone, 'He hated me. My mother knew he did, and that's why she took me away from Balmore when my father died. She didn't trust Alec. But I had to come back here after she'd died. Something drew me here. Perhaps it was the Highlander's attachment to his heritage. Who knows?' He shrugged and turned to face her again, his eyes dark and brooding as their glance lingered on her face. 'I came here. I met you. I fell in love with you one evening at twilight.'

'No, you didn't. You only pretended to be in love with me,' Kirsty retorted. 'You didn't really care about the real person who was me. You were in love with a fantasy woman.' She drew a shaky breath and held out her hand. 'Give me the key, please. I'd like to go now. I promised Hussein I would dine with him and his guests this evening and I'd like to change my clothes.'

'He invited me to dinner too,' he replied coolly. 'At seven, and it's now only five-thirty. We have plenty of time to finish this heart-to-heart talk, and at the risk of boring you I have to repeat that I fell in love with you and was foolish enough to believe you fell in love with me. I was even crazy enough to think of asking you to marry me one day when I'd become established as a surgeon in New York and you had graduated.' Kirsty made a short exclamation of disbelief and his eyes narrowed. 'Don't you believe me?' he queried sharply.

'No, I don't. How can I believe you? You went away without saying anything. You didn't write to me. There was nothing, only silence, blankness. It was as if you'd never existed,' she retorted stubbornly. 'If you'd cared, really cared about me, you wouldn't have left like that without saying anything, without even leaving a message for me.'

'But I did leave a message for you. I left a letter for you with Alec.' Neil stepped towards her, his eyes searching her face. 'I had to go away—suddenly, I admit, to New York, for an interview. It was the chance of a lifetime, one I couldn't pass up. I went to the Lodge to find you, to tell you I was leaving. You were out somewhere on the estate. I saw Alec instead. We had an interesting conversation.'

'What about?'

'About the fickleness of women in general and of my mother and you in particular,' he said dryly.

'Me?' she exclaimed. 'Alec said I was fickle? Oh, how ridiculous! You're making it up.'

'No, I'm not. I'm telling you exactly what we talked about. I told him of the interview in New York and of how I hoped to work with Carl Weingarten, the famous American orthopaedic surgeon. Alec was very enthusiastic and encouraging and said it was what my father would have wanted for me. Then I told him I wanted to marry you.' His lips twisted wryly. 'That was when he delivered his lecture on how fickle women could be. He told me that he hoped to marry you too and that you'd given him every reason to believe that you would once you'd graduated.'

'Every reason? What do you mean by every reason?' gasped Kirsty.

'You know damned well what I mean,' he retorted scornfully. 'You made love to him, made him think you loved him, just as you made me think you loved me. He said he'd thought of warning me about your fickleness but had hesitated.'

'I don't believe you,' she whispered, staring at him in horror. 'I don't believe Alec would say that about me.'

'But he did,' said Neil, his voice drawling wearily as if he were tired of trying to explain to her. 'Although I didn't believe what he said about you at the time and I said so to his face. He became angry then and challenged me to leave a letter proposing marriage to you since I didn't have time to see you before I left. He said he was sure you would turn me down. I wrote the letter then and there, sitting at his desk. He called Mary Taggart in and instructed me to give the letter to her to give to you. Then I left.'

'I didn't receive it. Mary didn't give it to me,' she moaned. 'Oh, I wish you'd stop telling lies! I wish you'd stop!' she cried, her hands holding her head as she shook it from side to side.

'I am not telling lies,' he snapped. 'Oh, come on, Kirsty, if Mary didn't give it to you she must have put it in your room at the Lodge. She's as honest and straightforward as anyone I know. She would make sure you got it somehow.'

'I'm not pretending—I didn't receive it,' she insisted.

'Okay, have it your own way if it makes you feel better, takes the edge off your guilt,' he sighed wearily, turning away from her again.

'I'm not guilty of anything,' she stormed. 'How do I know you wrote a letter to me? This is the first I've heard of it. Alec never told me about it. You could be pretending you wrote it to clear your conscience.'

'Hell!' Neil swore viciously, and paced towards the window, then swung round and paced back to her. His face was pale, his eyes glittered and he was breathing hard. 'For the last time I'll tell you. I wrote a letter to you proposing marriage and asked you to write to me at an address in New

York. When you didn't answer my letter I decided that Alec had been right about you after all and from then on I put my career first always. Women went way down to the bottom of my list of priorities.' He shrugged, his lip curling. 'It's paid off— I've been successful and made money.' He laughed shortly. 'I've never thought about it before, but I could say I owe my success and my wealth to you. You turned me down and helped to make me what I am now.'

'No, no,' she muttered, not wanting to take the blame for his hard cynicism where women were concerned. 'I didn't turn you down, because I didn't receive your letter. If I'd received it I'd have replied to it and then everything would have been different.' Her voice faded away to a whisper as the cold chill of regret crept along her veins. 'Oh, what's the use of talking about it, if neither of us believes what the other is saying and the only person who might have known the truth is dead?'

He looked up sharply as he slid his arms into the sleeves of his jacket.

'Alec, you mean?' he queried.

'Yes.' She sighed. 'When I asked him if he knew where you'd gone he said he'd almost warned me about you. He said you were like your father and that your morals where women were concerned were not of the best. He said you wouldn't come back and that I wouldn't hear from you again. And he was right. You didn't come back and I didn't hear from you again, and whatever there was between us soon died. It can't have been much, because it didn't stand the test of time and distance, did it? It's over.' She laughed a little, shrugging her shoulders. 'Once you were out of my sight you were soon out of my mind, Neil,' she lied. 'Could I have the keys now, please?'

He came towards her slowly and dropped the bunch of keys into her hand. She turned and inserted the key in the lock.

'But I did come back,' he said quietly behind her. The lock clicked as the key turned. She pulled the door open. 'I've come back, and it isn't over, whatever there was between us,' he added.

Kirsty glanced at him warily. There was an enigmatic slant to his lips and his eyes gleamed with his intention as he looked at her mouth deliberately.

'It's begun again,' he said softly, leaning towards her so that his breath caressed her lips tantalisingly. 'It's begun again in this love-nest where my father used to bring my mother.'

He slid an arm around her waist to draw her closer to him, yet still his mouth didn't touch hers but hovered tormentingly, and it came to her than that he was well aware of the power he possessed to rouse her to delirious abandoned passion. The realisation gave her strength and she pushed free of him.

'No, it hasn't begun again. It's dead, cold as ashes,' she said defiantly.

'Not quite dead. There are still a few embers left.' He touched her cheek lightly, his fingers sliding down to crook under her chin. 'And it'll be better this time, Kirsty, because we're both older, more knowledgeable. We're two consenting adults free to love where we wish.'

She knocked his hand away and backed out through the doorway.

'I'm not consenting to do anything with you,' she retorted, 'so you needn't think you're going to have an affair with me to pass the time this summer while you stay at Cairn Rua. You can find some other woman to be unfaithful to your wife with!'

'You're on the wrong track, Kirsty,' he said warningly, his eyes beginning to glitter angrily again. 'I wish you'd listen to me. . . .'

'I'm tired of listening to your lies, and I wish you hadn't come back!' she almost shouted at him. 'The sooner you leave again and go back to New York the better I'll feel. And don't forget to take the paintings. They're over there.'

She pointed across the room to the chest of drawers where she had put the paintings, and when he turned to look she left the room and ran down the winding stairway.

The kitchen was bright with light and noisy with the jabber of Arabic as Hussein's cook issued instructions to his helpers. Ahmed was leaning against the wallboard where the keys were hung watching all that was going on, but when he saw Kirsty he straightened up and came towards her.

'Have you locked the door?' he queried.

'No. Mr Dysart is still up there. I left the keys with him. Excuse me,' she said.

She slid past him and went out of the kitchen to leave the house by the side-door. Across the courtyard she walked, lifting her face to the soft drizzle of rain. There were two other cars in the yard, a big black Cadillac limousine which she presumed had brought Hussein's new guests and a sleek grey Jaguar which she guessed belonged to Neil. It was quite different from the battered little car he had driven four years ago, she thought with a bleak smile of remembrance. Quite different.

But then he was not successful and wealthy. *You turned me down and helped to make me what I am today*, he had said, and the bitterness in his voice had seared her. Kirsty's footsteps quickened and she hurried towards the factor's house, eager now to reach its quietness and privacy, to be alone for a while and sort out her thoughts. Neil had accused her also of being on the wrong track. But then hadn't he been wrong about her too?

In the house she went straight up to her bedroom intending to change her clothes, but once she had closed the door she gave way to her feelings. Flopping down on the side of the bed, she covered her face with her hands. Her heart was beating so hard it seemed to fill her throat and she felt sick. Sick at heart? Oh, God what was she going to do?

Moaning, she swayed back and forth in an agony of frustration and regret; regret for what might have been for the long-lost years when she and Neil could have been together if only she had received his letter, because if she had received his letter she would have answered it. Immediately. And she would have accepted his proposal of marriage. She would have given up all idea of getting a degree and of having a career. She would have flown to New York to live with him there, married or not.

She groaned again. Had he really written a letter to her? Only one person could verify the truth of his statement—Mary Taggart. The housekeeper might also know what had happened to the letter. Kirsty's hands slid from her face and she rose to her feet to move heavily and lethargically over to the wardrobe. In the long mirror she watched curiously as she approached her reflection.

With her hair down and tied at the nape of her neck she resembled the young woman she had been four years ago, Kirsty Ure, shy and sensitive, warm-hearted and romantic, longing to be loved and in love with a handsome rakish doctor. It was only when she got close to the mirror that she could see the droop to the corners of her mouth, the pinched look about her nose, the lack of sparkle in her eyes. She looked unhappy, down-right miserable, in fact. Unhappy Christina Whyte, who knew all about planting trees and looking after the land and who had done what her crippled husband had wanted, made Balmore the perfect example of how an estate should be managed. Oh, yes, she had been successful too, in her own way. But at what a cost!

She covered her face again and leaned against the wardrobe, her whole body shaking as forgotten emotions and sensations tore her apart. She wanted Neil with a hunger that frightened her. She ached for him and she could have had him. She could have found the physical satisfaction she had denied herself during the years of marriage to Alec with Neil this afternoon gloriously and tumultuously, and the embers of their love might have been rekindled into a new blaze.

So why hadn't she? Because Ahmed had interrupted them? No, that wasn't the reason. She and Neil could have continued to make love after Ahmed had gone. Then why had she rejected Neil's attempts to kiss her again?

She didn't trust him, that was why. She was afraid he would hurt her again. After all, he was married and would probably return to his wife once his holiday at Balmore was over. Feeling calmer, Kirsty pushed away from the wardrobe, and opened its door to flick through her clothing, her mind busy with new questions.

Why had Neil returned to Balmore alone? Had he really been drawn by something stronger than his will, by that primitive historic urge of the Highlander to return to his heritage? She paused in her search for another dress to wear, feeling exhausted suddenly, wondering whether she should send a message to Hussein asking to be excused because she had a headache so that she could avoid meeting Neil again that evening.

No—she braced her shoulders and lifted her chin—to do that would be to admit she was afraid of the power Neil possessed to disturb her. She must pretend she didn't care if he were there or not. She would put on the plain red silk jersey dress, make up her face, coil up her hair, tilt her lips into a smile and go over to the Lodge as if nothing unusual had happened to her that day.

She was a little late arriving in the lounge and she apologised politely to Hussein, who greeted her warmly, taking her hand in both of his while his dark eyes gleamed with admiration of her appearance. Keeping hold of her hand, he drew her into the room where his guests were sipping sherry.

Neil was there talking with one of the new-comers, a tall stately man with a lean swarthy face and a hooked nose who wore the traditional Arab headdress with his beautifully tailored pearl grey suit. Camille stood beside Neil looking up at him in blatant adoration. In a dress of apricot-coloured chiffon, which had an uneven petal-like skirt, she managed to look both childlike and sophisticated at the same time, and Kirsty felt envy crawl through her.

'I am wondering a little, Christina, why you did not tell me that your late husband's half-brother is a highly respected surgeon in the United States,' said Hussein as he handed her a glass of sherry.

'To tell the truth I'd forgotten about him,' she replied.

'You did not know, then, that he was coming here this month?'

'No. Alec, my husband, and Neil did not correspond with each other and I was very surprised when Neil walked into the gallery,' she said. And it was partly true. She had been surprised because she hadn't expected Neil to come to the tea party after their quarrel in the cottage garden.

She sipped sherry and glanced again at Camille and Neil. Was it her imagination or was Camille standing even closer to him?

'Who is the gentleman talking to Neil now?' she asked. 'He looks important.'

'He is my uncle, Said al Dukar, and he is a religious leader in my country,' replied Hussein. 'I will introduce him to you presently. But first I would like to know if you and Neil Dysart are good friends?'

She gaped at him in surprise. He was watching her closely, almost possessively, as he stood very close to her.

'No. We hardly know each other and I haven't seen him for years,' she said.

'Yet when he entered the gallery and you went to greet him this afternoon he kissed your hand and whispered in your ear. Camille noticed too. "They have been lovers," she said to me.' Hussein gestured with his hands. 'The French have a way of sensing such things,' he added.

Kirsty's hand shook a little as she raised her glass; but she managed to keep her colour under control.

'Camille has a vivid imagination,' she retorted lightly. 'And she's only eighteen, at an age when a woman sees romance everywhere and believes in it.'

'What is this?' queried Hussein mockingly. 'Are you trying to tell me that you don't believe in romance or that you are too old for it? I do not believe you are, Christina.'

'But it's true. I don't believe in romance any more.'

'So why did you go with Neil to the turret and spend more than an hour with him there, behind locked doors if you are not good friends with him?' he queried jealously, and for a moment she was tempted to tell him sharply to mind his own business.

'Oh, I suppose Ahmed told you,' she said, forcing a laugh. 'Poor Ahmed, I'm afraid Neil was rude to him. You see, Neil isn't used to having every move he makes watched. I tried to explain to him that Ahmed was only doing his job when he came up to find out who was in the turret room. Neil and I were going through the contents of the room. Some of the things up there belonged to his mother and I feel he should have them.' She looked down at her empty glass. 'The sherry is good. Do you think I could have some more, please?'

'Of course.' He had the grace to look a little flurried because she had apparently caught him out being bad-mannered. 'And come with me,' he added, taking her arm. 'I'll introduce you to my uncle, now.'

Half an hour later, seated at the dining table between Said al Dukar on her left and Madame Delacroix on her right and directly opposite to Neil who was sitting between Camille and another elderly Arab who had come with Said, Kirsty wished she had sent her excuses to Hussein after all and had not come. Trying to ignore Neil while he and Camille whispered and laughed together was more difficult than she had anticipated. It meant she had to give her undivided attention to either Said, whose English was not of the best, or to Madame Delacroix who preferred to converse with Said's secretary, a tall slim Arab who had been educated in France.

After a while her neck began to ache from turning her head first this way and that and keeping it turned so that she didn't have to look at Neil. But in spite of her efforts her glance kept sliding surreptitiously across the table to him, drawn as if by a magnet, only to flit away from him as soon as he became aware of her stare and withdrew his attention from Camille to look across at her.

He and Camille were getting on together far too well, she thought, and remembered uncomfortably that she had told him to find another woman to be unfaithful to his wife with.

But surely he wouldn't choose a girl hardly out of her adolescence? Kirsty looked up sharply and across at Camille as if to warn her only to encounter Neil's hard mocking eyes. With slow deliberation he turned his head to look at Camille's pretty oval face, which was turned up to his as she talked to him. Kirsty's lips thinned. Her question seemed to be answered. Neil had chosen to encourage Camille!

At last the meal was over and they all strolled back to the lounge to have coffee, thick and black, served in tiny cups. All of them except Camille and Neil, Kirsty realised with a stab of jealousy, and looked round at the others, wondering if anyone had noticed the absence of the other two. Only Madame Delacroix seemed to have missed them and was frowning anxiously at the wide-flung double door of the lounge as if willing her daughter to appear. After a while there came the sound of dance music from the record player in Alec's study. Madame Delacroix's face relaxed slightly. She came across the room and sat down beside Kirsty.

'Camille loves to dance,' she said. 'And she has missed her disco friends while she has been here. I think perhaps she has found a partner in Dr Dysart.'

'Perhaps,' replied Kirsty stiffly.

The music being played on the record player was certainly not disco. Nor was it rock and roll, nor punk rock. It was an old-fashioned slow fox-trot, a sentimental ballad played on a trombone backed by a big band, one of Alec's collection of music from the forties and fifties.

Body contact dancing? Kirsty's lips curled in self-derision. How cynical she was becoming! And it was taking her all her time not to leap to her feet and march into the study to see what was going on there.

'If I'd known Camille likes to dance I could have arranged for her to go to Balvaig. There are often dances held in the village hall, especially in the summer for the summer visitors,' she said as pleasantly as she could.

'Thank you,' replied Madame Delacroix politely. 'But we do not allow Camille to mix with strangers, you know,' she added snobbishly. She glanced at the group of men who were standing before the fire-place obviously arguing about something. 'I am glad to have a few minutes to talk to you privately, Lady Whyte,' she continued. 'I think it is time you were told why Jacques and I have brought Camille to stay here. It is to arrange the marriage between her and Hussein.'

'Oh,' said Kirsty weakly, her hand going to her forehead. Hadn't she had enough surprises for one week? 'I didn't know that they are engaged to be married.'

'They are not engaged yet,' said Madame Delacroix. 'They have known each other for a long time, six years in fact, and we have hopes, Jacques and I, that one day they will marry. Before he was assassinated Hussein's father was beginning to show leniency towards the match, and Camille has agreed to adopt the Islamic faith.'

'But what about Hussein? How does he feel?' asked Kirsty, whose free-thinking attitude to love and marriage caused her to be amazed by Madame Delacroix's cut-and-dried approach to her own daughter's marriage.

'He is fond of her and we think he would have proposed marriage to her before this if he hadn't been plagued with political and business problems ever since his father was killed.' Madame heaved a sigh. 'It has been an anxious time for him and we were relieved when he invited us here. We

hope that he has at last come to a decision.'
Madame gave Kirsty a sidelong glance from beneath lids which were painted green. 'But we
cannot be sure. He seems to be fascinated by you,
now.'

'Oh,' said Kirsty again, opening her eyes wide.

'I tell Camille and my husband that Hussein's
infatuation with you will not last,' Madame
Delacroix went on. 'I tell them all,' here she
waved a plump white hand, on which many rings
glittered, in the direction of the other groups of
people, 'that he is only temporarily attracted to
you because you are different from any other
woman he has known before.'

Madame's toothsome smile was worldly-wise.
'As I'm sure you know, it is not uncommon for a
young man to be attracted to an older experienced
woman, especially if he is a little shy, as in the
case of Hussein.'

'But I'm not that much older than he is,'
retorted Kirsty indignantly, her eyes flashing.
'About two years at the most.'

'But you have been married already,' Madame
reminded her dryly. 'You are not innocent like
Camille is. *Ça ne fait rien*,' she made a dismissing
gesture. 'What matters is this. Hussein will get
over his infatuation more quickly if you show a
little less appreciation of his attentions.'

'And how can I do that, Madame?' Kirsty asked
silkily. She was becoming more than a little irritated by the French woman's patronising, snob-
bish manner.

'You could refuse his invitations to dinner and

refrain from holding long conversations with him. You could hold yourself aloof. It should not be too difficult for you.'

Kirsty was silent for a few moments as she struggled to control an urge to tell Madame Delacroix where she could go with her advice. At last she managed to say,

'I think the music has stopped.' She almost laughed at the anxiety that flashed across the other woman's face. 'I suggest you go and see what Camille is doing. My husband's half-brother has a reputation for dalliance and it could be that Camille's chances of marrying Hussein are much more endangered by any friendship she forms with Neil than they are by me.'

She didn't wait to see what Madame Delacroix would do but walked over to the group of men who were not arguing any more but were listening to an impassioned speech by Said al Dukar, who was looking very stern. Hussein was looking sullen and defiant and Monsieur Delacroix was looking as if he were at the end of his patience. Said's secretary and the elderly Arab were both still and quiet, seeming very interested in the pattern on the carpet while they listened.

'Excuse me, your Excellency,' Kirsty said quietly to Hussein. 'I must leave now. Thank you for a pleasant evening.'

'It was my pleasure,' he said stiffly, bowing slightly to her, his eyes avoiding hers. 'Goodnight, Lady Whyte.'

'Goodnight.' She smiled generally in the direction of the other men and they all nodded to her, barely polite, and all her antennae quivered warningly. They were behaving towards her as if they had heard something about her they didn't like.

She walked across the room towards the doorway feeling rather than hearing the silence behind her. In the hallway she almost walked into Madame Delacroix who was hurrying towards the lounge breathlessly.

'They aren't there,' she exclaimed. 'The record was going round and round and they were not there. Do you know where they have gone?'

'No, I'm afraid I don't,' snapped Kirsty, and turning away walked down the passage to the side door of the house.

The drizzle had stopped and clouds were being blown across the sky by a warm breeze. In the east the moon was rising. In the west light from the sun which had just set still lingered. There were only two cars in the courtyard now, her own and the Cadillac limousine which had brought Said al Dukar to Balmore. The grey Jaguar had gone.

A movement drew Kirsty's attention to the shadows by the garage doors. The tall massive figure of the ever-watchful Ahmed appeared.

'You are looking for Mr Dysart, my lady?' he asked smoothly. 'He had left. Mademoiselle was with him.'

'Thank you,' she replied coolly. 'Goodnight.'

On the still damp stone flags of the courtyard her high heels made a sharp skittering sound as she walked once again towards her haven, the factor's house. The pines behind the house made a soft soughing noise as the breeze ruffled them. Above the curve of the dark moors behind the trees a star twinkled in a band of pale green sky still lit by the setting sun. It was going to be a lovely moonlit summer night in the Highlands; a night to be spent with a lover not alone.

Where had Neil taken Camille? Had he taken her to the dance in the village where he had sometimes taken herself? where they had often danced to the music of the fiddle and accordion?

> 'Now the fiddler's ready let us all begin,
> So step it out and step it in,
> To the merry music of the violin,
> We'll dance the hours away.'

The words and music of *The Dashing White Sergeant* the well-known Scottish choral dance jangled through Kirsty's mind as she entered the house. But her heart wasn't dancing, nor was it singing. It felt heavy in her breast, like a lump of lead, as she yearned for the times she had danced with Neil and then had ridden with him in his old car back to the cottage on Cairn Rua, and she wished she was with him instead of Camille.

CHAPTER FIVE

THE afternoon was warm and sunny, with a fresh breeze ruffling the loch making the water glitter with specks of silver light. High in the sky puffy white clouds blown over from the sea sailed above the summits of purple-grey mountains and away from the glen.

Kirsty drove her car up the road to the Lodge and into the courtyard. She parked it neatly, got out and took her shopping bags from the back seat. She had spent all morning in Balvaig, visiting the bank and buying necessities from the few small shops. Then she had had lunch with her friend Jessie Craig, who had also been recently widowed when her husband, the local veterinary surgeon, had died in a car accident.

Almost a week had passed since the day of the tea-party in the gallery, and during that week Kirsty had managed to stay aloof from the people who were staying in the Lodge, not because she had wanted to please Madame Delacroix, but because of an innate desire not to become involved with Hussein's problems.

It hadn't been difficult to keep clear of Hussein and the others because she hadn't been invited again to dinner, nor had she been asked to accompany Hussein and his guests on any of the fishing trips Hamish had organised for them or on any of their other outings. But she had been aware of the comings and goings of the Rolls and the Cadillac, and only that morning she had seen Said al Dukar depart in the big black car to return to London.

She hadn't seen much of Neil either, at least not to talk to him, but she knew he was still at the croft of Cairn Rua because she had seen the grey shape of the Jaguar streaking along the lochside road several times and had passed it one day when she had been driving back from Balvaig. He had honked his horn and had raised a hand in greeting as his car had flashed past hers. She hadn't waved back, but she had caught a glimpse of a shining blonde head close to his shoulder. Camille had not waved either.

The knowledge that the French girl had been with him had bothered her for the rest of the day in spite of her attempts to shake it out of her mind. She had a feeling Neil was deliberately trying to cause trouble with Hussein. Several times she had been tempted to go over to his cottage to remonstrate with him and to tell him Camille was more or less engaged to marry Hussein.

But she hadn't gone because she was afraid of what might happen if she did go. She was afraid he might try to make love to her again as he had in the turret room and, if he did, she might not be able to control her own desires. She might 'give', as he had called it, and if she did that she would have no self-respect left. She would hate herself for behaving no better than she had behaved four years ago, when she had believed he had been in love with her and she had been so sure she had loved him.

It wasn't as if she was in love with him now, she thought as she put away the groceries. How could she possibly fall in love with a man who behaved the way he was behaving? Who was openly unfaithful to his own wife by making love to another woman? And who told lies about Alec, her late husband?

She slammed the cupboard door closed to give vent to the strong hostile feelings memories of Neil's behaviour in the turret room had aroused in her. She despised him. She hated him and she wished he would go away, go back to New York.

'Hallo there, Lady Whyte. Do you have a wee minute to spare?'

Mary Taggart's lilting voice broke in on her thoughts and leaving the kitchen she hurried out into the small hallway. Mary was standing just inside the front doorway.

'I thought I'd just drop by to tell you what's going on at the Lodge today,' Mary said, her reddish-brown eyes sparkling with excitement. There was nothing she liked better than to be the bearer of gossip. 'Ach, there's been such a fuss over there this morning, so there has!'

'Come into the office,' said Kirsty, leading the way into the small room at the front of the house. 'And sit down while you tell me. I hope the fuss isn't to do with anything you and Hamish had done.'

'Ach, no,' said Mary, settling down into the only armchair in the room. 'Ye ken that young

French woman, Miss Delacroix? Well, she's gone off.'

'Gone off?' exclaimed Kirsty, with visions of cheese which had gone mouldy or meat that had become high. 'What do you mean?' She leaned against the desk.

'She's gone off somewhere without telling her mother. Mind you, it's the third time in a week she's gone out without telling anyone where she was going,' said Mary. 'But this time she's packed her bags and taken them with her. Now, what do you think of that?'

'I don't know what to think,' said Kirsty vaguely, but she felt her heart sink as she remembered again seeing Camille sitting in the front of Neil's car when it had passed her on the road, two days previously.

'If you ask me what I think ... which you're not doing ... I think she's found a friend,' said Mary importantly. 'Someone near her own age she can have fun with. And I can't blame her for going. She must have been sick to death with being cooped up here with her parents, yon Sheikh and his Arab friends, having to mind her manners all the time and to dress up in her best clothes. It's not natural for a young woman of her age to have to behave like that. I wouldn't have liked it when I was that age. Nor would you.'

'No, I wouldn't,' murmured Kirsty, thinking back to when she had been eighteen. Free and independent she had been in her first year at university, enjoying her studies and making friends where she wanted to. Marriage had been far from her mind and she had never spared a thought for the future. She had been much too busy making the most of the present.

'If ye canna have fun while ye're young ye'll never have it or ye'll always be hankering after it, to my way of thinking,' Mary philosophised. 'I mind I didn't take too kindly to being at home with my parents when I was that age. I used to go out every evening to meet my friends. We'd go to the flicks or to dances. Ach, we had a fine time, so we did. Anyway, Mr and Mrs Delacroix were in a terrible way this morning and I wouldn't be surprised if you'll be hearing about it now that it's known you're at home. They'll be wanting to see you to find out what you know about it.'

'But I know nothing. I've hardly seen Miss Delacroix for a week. In fact, I haven't spoken to her since I was at dinner with the Sheikh and his uncle when she. . . .' Kirsty broke off frowning.

'When she what?' prompted Mary, leaning forward curiously.

'Nothing much. She disappeared after dinner and her mother didn't know where she'd gone.'

'She went to the dance in Balvaig with himself of Cairn Rua,' said Mary, looking self-important again.

'How do you know?'

'Archie Thornton was playing the fiddle at the dance as he always does, and he told his wife Maggie that he was so surprised when he saw Neil Dysart that he nearly fell off the stage. But he was pleased too when Neil remembered him and had a few words with him. Archie said Neil had a young woman with him and told Maggie she was very pretty and had a lot of shining blonde hair. I guessed at once who she was when Maggie told me that.' Mary nodded again with an air of satisfaction with her own powers of deduction and rose to her feet. 'Ach, it's time I was off to my own place,' she said.

'Wait a minute,' said Kirsty as she followed the housekeeper into the hall. 'There's something I've been wanting to ask you. What's your memory like?'

'Fair to middling, I'd say,' replied Mary. 'I've a good memory for faces, but I'm not good at remembering names.'

'What about events, happenings? Could you remember something that happened four years ago, for instance?'

'Ach, now that might depend on what it was that happened if it was out of the usual run of things, ye ken.' Mary cocked her head to one side and looked at Kirsty out of the corners of her eyes. 'Four years ago, hm? What time of the year?'

'In the late summer. About the end of August.'

'You were here then, weren't you?'

'Yes, it was the first summer I had come to help Sir Alec. He was writing his book on Natural History.'

'Aye, I remember you arriving. Ye were a wee bit shy and didn't have much to say. Looked as if you wouldn't say bo to a goose,' Mary laughed. 'Who would have thought you'd turn out to be so clever and become Lady Whyte of Balmore? Aye, ye've done well, so ye have, and ye were a good wife to Sir Alec, God rest his soul. I mind him saying to me once he never regretted the day he married you, even though you were half his age.' Mary's expression became sardonic. 'I didn't like to tell him *he* was the lucky one when you agreed to marry him because he didn't have that many women to choose from. But ye didn't say anything like that to Sir Alec. Very sensitive about his handicap, he was.'

'You'll remember perhaps that Neil Dysart was also staying at his croft that summer,' said Kirsty, quickly getting a few words in edgeways while Mary paused to draw breath.

'Aye, I remember that too.' Mary gave Kirsty another sly sidelong look. 'You and he were awful friendly, I'm thinking.'

'He left at the end of that August, went away to New York,' persisted Kirsty stonily.

'So he did, so he did.' Mary's eyes narrowed as she seemed to look into the past. 'I mind he came to see Sir Alec before he left. I showed him into the study. They had an argument. I remember being a wee bit worried hearing Sir Alec shouting. I thought he might bring on another heart attack.' Mary's eyes focused on Kirsty's face. 'He'd had one before that summer, ye ken. That was when the doctor recommended he should employ someone to help him with his books and his plans for the estate.'

'But he didn't have a heart attack the time he was arguing with Neil, did he?' said Kirsty, determined to put Mary back to that particular moment in time.

'No. He quietened down and they parted

friends. I was in the room at the time and saw them shake hands. Neil gave me a letter for you and asked me to give it to you. Then he left.'

'But you didn't give me the letter,' said Kirsty. She felt suddenly short of breath with excitement as if she was on the verge of making an important discovery.

'I didn't need to. Sir Alec said he would give it to you when you came in. Aye, that's so—I remember him taking it from my hand.' Mary sighed. 'Now what was it you were wanting me to remember?' she asked.

'Oh, I just wondered if you could remember when Neil was here last, that's all. I wasn't sure whether it was that summer four years ago or whether he'd visited Balmore again, later that year, perhaps.'

'As far as I know he hadn't been back until now,' said Mary, opening the front door. Kirsty followed her out into the breezy sunny day. 'Ach, here comes the bodyguard,' she added. 'He'll be coming to summon you to appear before the Sheikh, I shouldn't wonder, so I'll be off. See you tomorrow.'

Mary hurried away and Ahmed approached, a dark alien figure.

'His Excellency would be pleased if you would agree to have tea with him on the terrace this afternoon,' he said, bowing slightly.

'Will anyone else be there?' Kirsty asked cautiously.

'I do not know, my lady. His Excellency said to tell you it is most important that you come.'

'Please tell him I'll be there in a few minutes,' she said, and with another bow he turned and walked back to the Lodge.

Fifteen minutes later, having changed from the suit she had worn for shopping into a flower patterned cotton skirt and a thin white cotton blouse, Kirsty stepped out of the French windows of the lounge on to the stone terrace.

'His Excellency won't be a moment,' Ahmed explained. 'Please take a seat.' He pulled out one of the wrought iron garden chairs from the small round table.

Sitting down, Kirsty tried to relax and enjoy the view. She had sat in this place on sunny afternoons sometimes with Alec but mostly by herself, and she would miss the view of the loch and the hills beyond if she ever had to leave Balmore; if she ever had to sell the estate, and the likelihood of her having to sell it once Alec's will had passed probate was looming larger and larger, judging by the letter she had received from his lawyer that week which had informed her that the mortgagers were threatening to foreclose if the debt was not paid off before the end of the year.

Why had Alec left such a financial mess? Why hadn't he told her he was so much in debt? What had she ever done to him that he had had to punish her in this way? Had he known she hadn't loved him? Had he guessed she had married him only because she had been sorry for him?

Her parents and her brother Duncan hadn't approved of her sudden marriage. Her mother in particular had been very much against it, and ever since relations between them had not been comfortable.

'It won't be normal, that's why,' Catherine Ure had replied when Kirsty had asked her why she hadn't approved. 'Don't you see? There's more to marriage than being a companion to a man old enough to be your father—much more. By tying yourself to Alec Whyte you'll miss a lot. You'll miss the joy of loving a man properly, of making your own home with a loving partner and of having children.'

'From what I've seen of some of my friends' marriages making a home, keeping house and coping with children aren't joy,' Kirsty had pointed out dryly. 'And some of them are wishing they hadn't opted for marriage but had stayed single and had continued with their careers. And their partners have turned out to be not all that loving. By marrying Alec I'll be able to continue with my career.'

'Marriage is a joy if you love your husband sincerely and he loves you,' Catherine had argued determinedly from the security of knowing that her own marriage had been successful and happy. 'By working together you can make it a joy.' Her blue eyes had expressed deep concern. 'Kirsty, I wish you would take more time to think about this. Leave Balmore, come home, or better still, look for a job somewhere else where you'll be with people your own age. You've been cut off from the reality of life, living up there in that romantic glen.'

'I like living there,' Kirsty had argued. 'And it's not true that I've been cut off from reality.

And I'm not going to leave and look for a job somewhere else. I'm going to stay there and I'm going to marry Alec.'

'You'll be sorry,' Catherine had remarked quietly.

'I don't think so,' Kirsty had retorted stubbornly.

'Isn't there another man you know whom you could marry, someone younger, someone you're in love with?' Catherine had queried shrewdly. 'I had a feeling last year that you'd met someone.'

'I did, but he went away and he's married to someone else now,' Kirsty had replied stiffly. 'And . . . and I don't think I'll ever be able to trust a man again. At least I won't be worried about Alec ever looking at another woman,' she had added miserably. 'He . . . he won't be unfaithful to me ever, for the simple reason that he's too crippled now. I'll always know where he is.'

'Kirsty, that's a terrible thing to say!' Catherine had remonstrated sharply. 'And not a good reason for marrying him.'

'I also admire and respect him, Mother,' she had retorted. 'Surely you approve of that? Oh, don't worry about me. I'll make it work out all right.'

And her marriage to Alec had worked out all right, she thought now. She couldn't say she had been unhappy during the two and a half years they had been married. She couldn't say either that she had been ecstatically happy. But then she had not expected to be, nor had she wanted to be. In her limited experience ecstasy was only followed by an aftermath of deep depression. She

had known ecstasy briefly with Neil, then he had
left her and for a long time afterwards the world
had been a grey dull place where she had moved
about like a robot, without feelings.

Alec had loved her in his own way, she was
sure. Then why hadn't he told her about his
debts? And why hadn't he told her about Neil's
letter? She didn't doubt that Mary Taggart had
told her the truth. It had all come out so naturally
and it meant that Neil had been telling her the
truth too. He had left a letter for her, a letter in
which he had asked her to marry him even though
Alec had told him she was fickle.

'Ah, forgive me, Christina. I did not intend to
keep you waiting.'

Hussein had stepped out on to the terrace. Slim
and dark, as neatly dressed as ever, he pulled out
another chair from the table and sat down. A
young Arab, one of the helpers from the kitchen,
appeared with the tea tray and set it down. When
that was done he stood waiting politely until
Hussein dismissed him.

'Please pour the tea, Christina,' Hussein said.
The tray was set only for two.

'No one else is coming?' she asked, lifting the
silver pot.

'No. I wished to see you alone. It seems a long
time since we talked last. There have been too many
people, too many problems.' He sighed. 'I have
missed you and it is good to be with you again. In
your presence I always feel I can relax, be myself.'

'I noticed that your uncle left this morning,'
she said, placing a cup and saucer before him.

'Yes. And I am glad he has gone.' Immediately he bit his lip. 'I should not say that because I realise he has only been trying to do what he sees as his duty.' He sighed again. 'Since my father was killed Uncle Said feels he must advise me on all matters, not just political and business matters but personal and religious ones too.' He picked up the tea cup and sipped from it. 'He did not like me being friendly with you, Christina, and so while he was here I did not invite you to come to the house again or to go out with me. You understood, I hope.'

'Yes, of course I did. I suppose he didn't like you being friendly with me because I'm a Christian,' she said. 'I remember you saying that your father didn't like you to associate with women who are not of your faith.'

'No. It was not that.' His dark glance wavered away from her. 'Uncle Said was with me when Ahmed told me about finding you in the turret with Dr Dysart. He could not help overhearing what Ahmed said to me and I'm afraid he got the impression that you are. . . .' Hussein broke off, dull red staining his sallow cheeks. 'I do not like to say this, Christina, but my uncle felt that perhaps you are a woman who is too free with her favours.'

Hussein flushed even more with embarrassment and Kirsty sat perfectly still, staring at him.

'What exactly did Ahmed tell you?' she asked after a while, her voice dangerously smooth.

'He said that it looked very much to him as if you and Neil had been lying on the bed together,' muttered Hussein.

'Is that all he said?' asked Kirsty, quelling an urge to burst out laughing suddenly.

'Yes.'

'And you believed him, of course.'

'I didn't want to, but my uncle did,' he murmured. 'But let us forget what Ahmed said and what my uncle inferred from it. I have to tell you that Monsieur and Madame Delacroix are now very upset. You know, of course, that last week when you came to dinner, Neil took Camille to the dance in Balvaig.'

'I did hear about it.'

'And every day since then Camille has left the house without telling anyone and has gone either to his cottage or out in his car?'

'How do you know this?' Kirsty asked. 'Has Camille told you she'd been meeting Neil?'

'No. She has told me nothing. She has been strange, a little wild, and when her mother has remonstrated with her, she has answered insolently, refusing to say where she has been or to give the name of the person she has been meeting. She has not been like Camille at all, but like a woman who has been suddenly bewitched.' Hussein shook his head slowly from side to side. 'I do not understand her any more.'

'She could have been meeting someone else, a young man she met at the dance, perhaps,' said Kirsty, wondering whom she was trying to convince, Hussein or herself, that Camille had not been meeting Neil, 'It isn't unusual for a girl of her age to want the company of people of her own age. It must have been dull for her staying her, especially after Paris.'

'She has been meeting Neil,' insisted Hussein. 'She has been seen walking up to his cottage and has been seen in his car.'

'Have you seen her with him?'

'No, but Ahmed. . . .'

'Of course,' said Kirsty scornfully. 'Ahmed. He sees everything, doesn't he? He makes it his business to see everything and report back to you. He's nothing but a spy and a busybody, and I'm still angry with him for telling you I was with Neil in the turret for an hour behind a locked door and for implying what he did. It was none of his business what we were doing. It was none of yours, either.'

'Please, Christina,' Hussein said reproachfully, 'do not be angry with me. I didn't want to believe what he implied. I didn't want to believe my uncle either. I like you.'

He broke off with a muttered imprecation and springing to his feet paced over to the stone balustrade which edged the terrace. For a moment he stood staring out at the loch, then he turned to face her, resting his hips against the balustrade. Even at that distance she could sense the tension which was in him.

'Can you deny what Camille suspects?' he asked tautly, his dark eyes seeming to burn into hers. 'Can you deny that you and Neil Dysart were once lovers? And can you deny that you and he were making love in the turret room when Ahmed knocked on the door?'

His questions caught her off guard. Pink colour suffused her face, but pride and a certain hard-won dignity came to her aid.

'As I've said, it's none of your business,' she replied coolly, and rose to her feet. 'I think it's time I left, if that's all you have to say to me.' She turned towards the window.

'No, please, Christina—wait!' He hurried to her side. 'That isn't all I have to say to you. In fact that isn't what I wanted to say at all. Ah, in the name of Allah, will you please listen? This morning Camille left the house very early before anyone was awake and she took all her belongings with her in her suitcases.'

'Has she gone back to France?' Kirsty asked, turning obligingly to face him.

'We do not know where she has gone. But we know with whom she has gone,' he replied grimly. He pushed a hand into his jacket to an inside pocket and brought out a single sheet of thick writing paper. He handed it towards her. 'Read it,' he ordered.

Kirsty took the note, opened it and looked down at the sloping writing. She recognised only three words: Hussein, Neil and Camille. She handed it back to Hussein.

'It's in French,' she said. 'I can't read it. Please tell me what it says.'

He took the note from her, his face set in grim lines.

'It says, "My dear Hussein. I can't stand it any longer. Please try to understand. I have gone with Neil Dysart. My love to you always. Camille." That's all. Not a word of where they have gone.'

Kirsty felt suddenly the need for support and

put her hand out to the back of the chair she had just vacated. In the silence she could hear the lap of water on the shore, the sigh of wind in the trees, the sound of a lawn mower from the back of the house.

'You do not seem very shocked or surprised,' Hussein said. 'Did you know? Did your "lover" Neil tell you he was taking Camille away with him?' he demanded hoarsely.

'No. I knew nothing about it. And Neil is not my lover and I have no knowledge of his plans,' she retorted.

'So you do not know where he might have taken her?'

'No.' She paused, then added more gently, 'Hussein I'm really sorry this has happened.'

'In the way perhaps that you were really sorry when he stole my Rolls and helped his friends to escape?' he replied viciously. 'You knew all the time he had helped them, yet you said you were sorry.'

'They weren't real poachers,' she objected. 'They were two young men on holiday, enjoying themselves. And they put the fish back. They were only trying to prove to Neil that they could catch a fish by that method.'

'But you knew they were his friends and you pretended you were sorry my car was stolen,' he accused her.

'I didn't pretend,' she said. 'I was sorry at the time because you were so upset. And I'm sorry now because you're obviously upset Camille has left with Neil. I wish I could do something to help, but I can't. I don't know what to do.'

'Aah!' Hussein clutched his head between his hands. 'I think I will go mad,' he muttered wildly. 'Your calmness will drive me mad! You do not seem to understand. The woman I am considering for marriage has gone away with another man who is your erstwhile lover. Why aren't you furiously angry as I am? Do you not care for Dysart?'

'Look, I am a little worried, I must admit, on Camille's behalf,' she said. 'I mean, she's so young and has led such a sheltered life. But she's old enough to make her own decisions, to choose what she wants to do, and perhaps she has chosen to have a little fun before she settles down to marriage with you and life in your harem. I can't say I blame her. Living in a harem must be like living in prison.'

Hussein's face went red again and the veins stood out on his forehead while his black eyes glared at her.

'I will not have a harem,' he said through gritted teeth. 'I loathe the institution. I shall have only one wife. But she must be innocent, untouched, when I marry her, as I know Camille to have been until now.' He gasped as if short of air and made a few rapid paces back and forth in front of her. 'But now,' he muttered as he stopped to face her again, 'now she has gone with Dysart I cannot be sure of her any more. You yourself told Madame Delacroix he has a reputation for amusing himself with women, and who should know that better than you?'

'Oh dear, yes I did say that, didn't I?' said Kirsty, biting her lower lip. She was experiencing again a desire to burst out laughing in reaction to Hussein's excitability. He seemed to be making such a fuss about very little. 'I'm so sorry,' she began again. 'No, you don't like me to say that, do you? But what else can I say? What are you going to do? I'm surprised you haven't sent Ahmed after them?'

'By the time I had found the note and we had realised Camille had gone it was too late,' said Hussein, calming down. 'Monsieur and Madame Delacroix have gone to Fort William this afternoon to the police station to lay charges against Dysart.'

'Charges of what?' exclaimed Kirsty.

'Kidnapping.'

'Oh, no! They can't do that!' All desire to laugh had gone. She was really worried about Neil. 'Camille has gone with him of her own free will. The fact that she's taken all her belongings with her proves that.'

Hussein gave her a dark suspicious glance.

'I suppose it does,' he muttered grudgingly. 'But, in the name of Allah, what am I going to do? My uncle, who is the chief leader of the Islamic faith in my country, has just given me permission to ask Camille to marry me because she had promised to change her religion, and now she has run away!'

'Go after her,' suggested Kirsty brightly.

'But I don't know where they have gone. If I knew I'd have followed them by now.'

'Then you'll just have to wait won't you? I'm sure she'll let her parents know where she is sooner or later.'

'That is all you have to say?' he whispered.

'That's all.'

He stared at her, his face working with conflicting emotions, then stepped forward and grasped her hands in his to hold them close to his chest.

'Christina, I love you,' he whispered. 'I love your eyes, your skin, your hair. I love your soft musical voice. I love the way you laugh, the way you sigh. I love your cool clear mind. I love you more than I love Camille, so what are you going to do about it?'

Amazed, she stared up into the soft black eyes for a moment, then tried to free her hands, afraid that Ahmed or one of the other security men might appear.

'Hussein, you're distracted with worry and you don't know what you're saying,' she replied. 'Please let me go.'

'No. And I do know what I'm saying. And if circumstances were different I would ask you to marry me now that Camille has gone.'

'Circumstances? What circumstances? What do you mean? Are you sure you're using the right word?' she asked.

'You have been married. You are a widow. You are no longer a virgin, and the woman I must marry must be. . . .'

'Innocent. Untouched,' she said dryly. 'I see.' She tried again to free her hands, but his grasp tightened.

'Wait,' he ordered. 'Hear me out. I cannot marry you, but we could be lovers. You could be my mistress, live here all the time, and I could visit you. Ah, Christina, please say you will!'

Astounded by his suggestion, she stared at him again, recalling her own mocking remark that she might marry Hussein and use his money for Balmore.

'You mean you'd continue to pay rent for Balmore and allow me to live here if I agree to be your mistress?' she whispered.

'That is exactly what I mean. Or if you would prefer it I will buy Balmore from you and give it back to you as long as I could visit you here and be assured of a welcome when I come.' He pressed closer to her, his dark face hovering just above hers, his dark eyes blazing. 'I love you and I want you to be mine. Never have I felt like this about a woman. Christina, you must say yes,' he pleaded. 'You must say yes!'

'I can't. I can't give you an answer, not yet. I . . . I'll have to think about it. Now please let me go. Someone might come and find us like this, see you holding me like this.'

'Ahmed might come, you mean.' His mouth twisted wryly. 'I wish he would come and find you in my arms. But he isn't coming, so I will continue to hold you like this, and now I am going to kiss you.'

His lips were hot, moist and soft. They pleaded

for her response rather than demanded it, and Kirsty kissed him back because she felt sorry for him and also because she thought that if she did he would release her.

'You see, you like me a little bit,' he said with a flicker of triumph as he let her go. 'You returned my kiss. But I will give you time to think about my proposition. Tomorrow you will give me an answer.' He looked past her and he frowned. 'What is it, Mohammed?'

Kirsty turned quickly. One of the bodyguards was standing just within the French window, his dark face impassive. He spoke to Hussein quickly in Arabic.

'It is my uncle phoning me from London,' Hussein explained to Kirsty. 'I tried to reach him earlier, but he was not at his hotel. Now he is returning my call. You will please excuse me while I talk to him?'

'Of course.'

'And you will wait here until I come back?' he asked. 'Have some more tea?'

'No. I have work to do. I'll see you tomorrow,' she replied, and turning, she walked away along the terrace and down the steps at the end.

She needed something a lot stronger than tea to soothe her, thought Kirsty wryly as she entered the factor's house again. A good tot of straight whisky wouldn't have done any harm, only she didn't drink and there was no whisky in the house. She possessed no means of seeking oblivion from her tumultuous thoughts.

But she couldn't spend the evening by herself.

She had to get out of the house, go somewhere. There was only one place where she knew she would be welcome. She would go to Jessie's house and tell her friend about Hussein's surprising proposition. She might even tell Jessie about her anxiety about Camille's apparent elopement with Neil.

Over an hour later, sitting in an armchair in Jessie's house on the outskirts of Balvaig, she told her everything.

'Well!' gasped Jessie. 'To think of you being asked to be the mistress of a real live Sheikh! It's like a story out of the Arabian Nights. Or a novel by Elinor Glyn or Ethel M. Dell.' Her dark brown eyes narrowed shrewdly. 'I can understand, though, why you're in a bit of a tizzy over that French girl running away with Neil Dysart. And you were right to come here and tell me about it. No good you bottling all that up inside yourself. Ach, some men are never happy unless they're causing trouble!'

'I'm only worried in case . . . in case he takes what he wants and then drops her,' sighed Kirsty, trying to ignore the feelings of jealousy which kept swelling up inside her. 'In case he hurts her.'

'As he hurt you, you mean, four years ago. I thought you'd got over that?' remarked Jessie.

'I had,' whispered Kirsty.

'Then forget him and her.'

'I can't. I keep wondering where he's taken her and what they're doing. Oh, Jessie how could he do it? How could he do it?' she groaned.

'Now you can stop that!' said Jessie sharply.

'No man is worth all this self-torture you're putting yourself through. You're not responsible for anything he does. And you're not going back to Balmore tonight. You can come with me to the party at the sailing club.'

'But I haven't been invited and I'm not a member.'

'That won't matter. You're coming with me and we'll have a good time. The fact that you're Lady Whyte of Balmore will be enough to open the doors wide to you.'

'Yes, but you know I don't like using the title. . . .'

'Shut up!' said Jessie, laughing. 'It's time you had some fun. Ever since Alec died you've been turned off. God knows why, because we all know you and he didn't. . . .'

'Didn't what?' Kirsty interrupted her threateningly.

'You know what I mean,' retorted Jessie with a knowing grin. 'Anyway, it's time you got into circulation again. You don't want to be a widow for ever, do you? So we'll go to the party, have a few drinks, get a little squiffed and maybe someone will ask us to dance. And don't worry about having to drive back to Balmore. You can stay the night here.'

'All right,' Kirsty capitulated suddenly, thankful that for the next few hours she wouldn't have a chance to worry. 'Do you think this skirt and blouse are suitable to wear?'

CHAPTER SIX

ALTHOUGH she hadn't gone to bed until the early hours of the morning Kirsty woke early next day and lay for a while drowsily looking around the small bedroom at the back of Jessie's house. Sunlight slanted in around the edges of the brightly coloured curtains which covered the dormer window. It was time she got up and went back to Balmore to find out if Hussein had heard from Camille.

Quickly she sat up, then groaned, her hands going to her head as pain twisted through it. Remembering how she had come by the headache, she grinned ruefully. She had drunk too much at the party, not a lot but too much for her because she wasn't accustomed to drink. But it had been a good party. She had enjoyed it. And she had met some pleasant people of all ages, mostly summer visitors who owned houses and cottages in or near Balvaig which they had renovated and had turned into comfortable holiday residences.

'Kirsty? Are you awake? I've brought some tea.'

Jessie pushed the door open. She came in carrying a tray on which there were two mugs and a teapot. She was wearing a flower-patterned quilted housecoat and her curly hair was tousled. She set the tray down on the bedside table, then perched on the edge of the bed. Her dark brown eyes quizzed Kirsty's face.

'How do you feel this morning?' she asked.

'Not bad, but I have a headache.' Kirsty reached out and lifting the teapot poured tea into the mugs. Picking up one of them, she drank some of the clear brown liquid without sugar or milk. 'Mmm, it tastes good,' she said, and glanced at her friend's round good-humoured face. 'I hope I wasn't silly or anything last night. I think I had too much to drink.'

'You had a bit more to say than usual, that's all,' said Jessie. 'Otherwise you were your normal lively self. And you were certainly a hit with some of the lads. I'm thinking they fall for those big blue eyes of yours.' Her glance swept over Kirsty. 'You know, you have all the makings of a *femme fatale*. There's an aura of mystery about you. No wonder the Sheikh has fallen for you and asked you to be his mistress! Have you decided what to do? Are you going to accept his offer?'

Kirsty finished her tea and set the mug down on the tray. Leaning back against the pillows, she folded her arms behind her head. She was wearing one of Jessie's nightgowns and it was several sizes too big for her. The bodice had slipped down to give a tantalising glimpse of her uptilted white breasts.

'No, I'm not,' she said firmly. 'Knowing me, can you imagine me as the mistress of a wealthy Arab, my favours bought and paid for?'

'No, quite frankly, I can't,' said Jessie, and her face expressed relief. 'You're too much of a puritan like me. And too damned independent. It has to be marriage or nothing for both of us.' Jessie laughed as she poured more tea. 'And the way things are going for me it looks as if it's going to be nothing! Not one of the men I've met recently can compare with Jamie.' She sighed, her eyes darkening with sadness. 'Oh, Kirsty, I do miss him,' she whispered, her eyes filling with tears.

Touched by her friend's distress, Kirsty spent the next few minutes comforting her. As she expected, Jessie soon cheered up and left the room to go downstairs to prepare breakfast.

It was nearly ten o'clock when Kirsty left the house and set off for Balmore. She drove fast along the winding road to Glen Lannach, hardly sparing a glance for the beauty of the scenery; the lush green meadows dotted with shaggy golden-brown Highland cattle; the light and dark pattern of larch and pines; the purple-tawny sweep of moorland; and towering over all the naked rain-scoured rocks of the mountains seeming to touch the clouds which were fast covering the sky.

The nervous agitation from which she had suffered the previous afternoon was back. She was worried still about what had happened. Why was she so anxious? She had told Jessie that it was on Camille's account she was worried, in case Neil hurt the girl, but she knew deep down that she didn't care what happened to Camille at all. It was on Neil's account she was worried. She was afraid of the damage he might do to himself by running away with Camille.

Since Camille came from an important French

family and had been staying with a well-known Arab there could be publicity about the elopement. In their attempts to find their daughter she guessed that the Delacroixs would have no hesitation in using the media to draw the attention of the British public to what had happened.

And adverse publicity would damage Neil's reputation as a surgeon. It would disrupt his marriage. It might destroy him!

Oh, why should she worry about him? Why should she care what happened to him? He had meant nothing to her for the best part of four years, so why feel deeply concerned about him now? Why did she have this urge to rush to his defence, to protect him against the consequences of his own mischievous behaviour? Surely she wasn't in love with him again? No. She shook her head in quick negation. It took time to fall in love, and she hadn't seen much of him since he had returned. It took time ... yet four years ago it had taken her only ten minutes!

By the time she reached the Lodge rain had begun to spit down from the grey clouds. Yet the yard was full of people coming and going, Hussein's Arab servants hurrying to and from the side door of the house, carrying out cases and boxes, packing them into the van in which they had travelled up from London and which had been parked in the middle garage ever since it had arrived.

Seeing Ahmed, Kirsty went over to him.

'What's happening?' she asked.

'We are leaving, my lady. His Excellency wishes

to see you as soon as possible. He is in the lounge.'

Hussein was sitting at the desk in the lounge talking on the phone. When he saw her he said a few more words, then put the receiver down. Rising to his feet, he did not approach her but waited for her to go to him. His face was serious, his dark eyes sad.

'Good morning, Christina,' he greeted her. 'All morning I have been looking for you. I looked for you last evening too, but you were not at your house.'

'I went to Balvaig to visit a friend, and stayed the night with her. Why did you want to see me?'

'To tell you I am going to look for Camille.'

'Oh, have you heard from her? Do you know where she is?'

'No, we haven't heard from her, but we think she is in London. Yesterday evening the Delacroixs received an anonymous phone call. The person who spoke to them said that Camille was safe and well and was staying with a friend near London, then hung up. They left immediately for London in their car. I said I would join them there today and help them to search for her.' He twisted his hands nervously together. 'I hope you understand why I must go.'

'Of course you must go and look for her. I understand.'

His hands stopped twisting. He looked at her, and relief shone in his eyes. His glance seemed to caress her.

'I knew you would understand,' he said. 'You

are a very generous and understanding person. A man feels comfortable with you and that is important. It is why I have fallen in love with you.' He stepped closer to her. 'Have you thought about my suggestion? You promised to give me an answer today.'

'Yes, I have thought about it,' Kirsty replied steadily. 'The answer is no. I couldn't do it. I'm not that sort of woman.'

To her surprise he nodded, although it seemed to her that tears glistened suddenly in his eyes.

'I expected you to answer in that way,' he said. 'As you say, you are not that sort of woman. You are the sort of woman who should be comfortably married to a kind, supportive husband, who should be bearing and rearing children.' He broke off, his face twisting with pain. 'I wish to Allah that I could be your husband. I wish I had the courage to run away from my responsibilities, turn my back on the Sheikhdom of Dukar, stay here and marry you, live with you here always. But I don't have the courage. I am afraid to offend my people, my uncle, the leaders of my religion.' He held out a slim dusky hand to her. 'This is goodbye, Christina. I will not be coming back to Balmore.'

'But you've paid the rent for six months!' she exclaimed.

'I know, but I will not be coming back. Now that I know I cannot have you I will not come back. You see, I could not bear to be here, to see you almost every day and knowing that I cannot ever give expression to my love for you.'

'I could be away when you want to stay here. You wouldn't have to see me,' she offered.

'No.' He shook his head. 'It is my destiny to marry another woman, if not Camille, then some other innocent girl who probably would not like this place any more than Camille does. This is the parting of our ways.'

'But you must let me refund the rent you've paid,' said Kirsty anxiously, knowing that the money had already been used to pay off some of Alec's debts. 'It's so wasteful to pay rent for a place you're not going to live in.'

'I can afford it,' he said with a shrug, then added in an agonised whisper, 'Please will you say goodbye and go, Christina. I can't bear being with you any longer.'

'Goodbye,' she said softly, and kissed him quickly on the cheek. 'I hope you find Camille none the worse for her adventure and are able to marry her.'

Leaving the lounge, she went to the kitchen to make sure Mary Taggart was there and supervising the departure of the Arab cook and his equipment. But the cook and his minions had already gone and Mary was alone, humming cheerfully to herself as she cleaned the big electric range.

'Well, I can't say I'm sorry they're leaving,' she said. 'And I won't be singing "Will ye no come back again" to them, either. Good riddance to them all!' she glanced sideways at Kirsty. 'Ach, ye're looking a wee bit pale this morning. I'll put the kettle on and we'll have a good cup of tea by way of celebration.'

Through the rain-spattered window Kirsty watched the van reverse into the space of the yard and then go forward and out of sight. A few seconds later the Rolls-Royce followed, driven by Ahmed with Hussein sitting beside him. Then that had disappeared too and there was only the soft tinkle of raindrops falling on the old grey cobbles of the yard and against the window pane.

'So that's that,' said Mary prosaically as she poured tea. 'And I'm thinking you won't be in a hurry to let the place to a foreigner again after that experience,' she added sharply.

'I'll have to let it to someone,' retorted Kirsty. 'Mary, do you have any aspirin? I've got an awful headache.'

'Ach, sure I have.' Mary went to a closet to find her handbag and rummage in it.

Kirsty sat with her shoulders slumped and her head in her hands, staring at the cup and saucer in front of her but not seeing it. Hussein had gone. The Delacroixs had gone. Neil had gone. Balmore was back to normal. She could move back into the Lodge if she wished, take up the usual routine, behave as if nothing strange had happened; as if the place hadn't been overrun with Arabs; as if Neil hadn't come back.

Where was he now? Was he in London with Camille? Oh God, she hoped not. She couldn't bear the thought of him making a fool of himself over an eighteen-year-old blonde. She ground her teeth and glared at the cup and saucer. She hadn't thought it possible to be so jealous. And possibly it was her own fault Neil had taken Camille away

with him. He might not have done it if she herself
had not rejected him in the turret room; if she
hadn't thrown a taunt at him.

*You can find some other woman to be unfaithful
to your wife with.* She groaned softly with regret,
wishing she had never said that. It had been a
mistake to taunt Neil like that. She should have
known better than to throw down a challenge in
front of him. Neil was the type of man who would
always take up a challenge. Descended from a long
line of stubborn, fighting Highlanders, he would
enjoy nothing better than to pick up the gauntlet
tossed before him and to throw it back in his
enemy's face.

'Here you are,' said Mary, plonking down a
small bottle of aspirin. 'Take some with your tea
and then be off with you for a rest. You look worn
out. It's been too much for you, the worry of this
place, and I for one wouldn't blame you if you
did get rid of it. You're too young to be saddled
with the responsbility of it. You should be off and
away, working with people your own age, enjoying yourself.'

'But you wouldn't like me to sell it to a foreigner,'
said Kirsty dryly after swallowing two aspirin.

'No, not to a foreigner,' replied Mary wisely.
'To someone who belongs to this country, even
an Englishman would do. There must be someone
who can afford to buy it.'

'Yes, there must be,' said Kirsty with a sigh,
rising to her feet. 'I'm going to spend some time
this afternoon in the study. I have to look for
something in there.'

The study, which had once been the hub of the house, had a musty unused atmosphere now. Pausing in the doorway, Kirsty tried to imagine what Alec had been doing the day Neil had come to look for him nearly ten years ago.

Alec would have been sitting as usual behind the big desk in his wheelchair, near to the window and his telescope. Slowly she closed the door and walked over to the desk. Alec would have watched anyone approaching him in silence, looking over the tops of his dark-rimmed reading glasses, his blue eyes wintry, his small mouth tightly pursed, his intention to reduce the person coming towards him to a state of awe and possibly fear. It had taken her a long time to find out that his rather bulldoggish, Churchillian pose had been just that, a pose; a defence behind which he had hidden his weakness and caused by his handicap.

But she doubted if Neil had been afraid of Alec. Neil would have advanced into the room as if he had owned it and would have marched right up to the desk and said outright what he wanted without waiting to be asked. And that day he had asked to see her.

Going over to the desk, Kirsty sat on the side of it, away from the window. The top of it was neatly set with a blotting pad, a sheaf of writing paper and some envelopes, put there for the use of the tenant of the house. In Alec's day the top would have been scattered with books and papers and he would have moved some of the books to give Neil room to write the letter to her.

When the letter had been written Neil had given

it to Mary Taggart. Then he had left. At Alec's request Mary had given the letter to him. Where had Mary put it? On the desk? Or into Alec's hand? If she had put it on the desk the chances were it had been covered up and forgotten, perhaps collected up with some papers and put somewhere else. Or it might have been thrown in the waste-paper basket and destroyed before Alec had remembered to give it to her.

She hoped that was what had happened. Now that she was sure that Neil had written the letter she didn't want to believe that Alec had deliberately withheld it from her.

Yet Alec had rarely mislaid anything. He had always tidied his desk himself at the end of the day, sorting out the correspondence he had received, filing the personal letters himself, putting the business letters in a pile to be filed later by her in the big filing cabinet.

She knew he had kept the few personal letters he had received in a locked box in his room. It was still there and several times she had thought she should go through it since he had died. But an innate dislike of prying into other people's privacy had kept her from unlocking the box. She should really open it, though, because there might be something in it of importance. *The letter Neil had left for her, perhaps?*

Oh, no. That was just wishful thinking. The letter was lost, gone for ever, swept away. Springing to her feet, she left the study and returned to the factor's house. The postman had been and there was a pile of bills on the doormat.

Kirsty picked them up and flicked through them quickly. Electricity, the half-yearly rates, a note from the Inland Revenue, and a letter from Dawson, Pettigrew and Tanner, family solicitors.

Going into the kitchen, she dropped the bills on the table and ripped open the letter from the solicitors. The letter was very short and to the point. It asked her to meet with a Mr Douglas Pettigrew at his office in Fort William at her earliest convenience to discuss the will of the late Sir Alec Whyte.

Chewing her lower lip, Kirsty re-read the note, wondering what lay behind the uncommunicative statement. Why should she discuss Alec's will with another lawyer? As far as she was concerned the will was quite straightforward. Alec had left everything to her. It was a proper legal document and had been drawn up with the help of Alec's own lawyer, Mr Robert Rankin, of Tweedie, Rankin and Peat, Glasgow.

She pushed the note back into its envelope, made herself some lunch and then went to the office. It was a good day to catch up on the correspondence and involving herself in estate work would as usual take her mind off personal problems. First of all she phoned the office of Dawson, Pettigrew and Tanner and made an appointment to see Mr Douglas Pettigrew, the next day. Then, sitting down, she pulled the rack where the letters she had received recently had piled up and began to go through them.

Two hours later she leaned back in her chair and stretched her arms. It was time to stop and do something else. Going to the window, she looked out. The rain had stopped and the clouds were clearing. Patches of blue sky showed. She would have her tea and then walk around the estate and call in to see some of the farmers as she usually did on a fine evening.

The sun had long been set and the moon was rising, peering above the summit of Cairn Rua when she walked up the slope to the dark and silent Lodge. As always the long walk had soothed her. She felt at peace with her world to-night and knew she would sleep well.

Before turning into the courtyard she paused to look down at the ghostly glimmer of the loch. Out of habit her glance lifted to the dark slopes of Cairn Rua and her heart skipped a beat. Narrowing her eyes, she stared intently. No, it wasn't her imagination. A yellow gleam of light twinkled through the bushes that surrounded the cottage. Someone was there. Neil? Had he come back? Or had someone broken in?

Almost before she realised it Kirsty was running down the road, her rubber boots clumping on the surface. Along the lochside road she hurried, her glance still held by the twinkle of light until it disappeared as she approached the far side of the loch and the cottage was hidden by the curve of the lower slopes of the hill.

Up the rough gravel road she walked, her speed slowing down as she reached the top of it. Breathless, she paused at the opening in the dry-stone wall, staring at the light slanting from the window and hearing the loud clamour of her heart in the soft still silence of the night.

Cautiously she approached the window. It was set low enough for her to see inside the living room. At the plain wooden table Neil was sitting. There was a sketch pad in front of him and a piece of charcoal between his fingers. But he wasn't sketching. His head supported by his left hand, his left elbow resting on the table, staring at the pad of paper as if thinking.

Relieved that it was he who was in the house and not an intruder, Kirsty stepped back from the window. She stepped on one of the stones which formed the edge of the flower bed under the window. Her ankle twisted and she lost balance. The large stone clattered against another stone, and she fell, knocking other stones together. The sound of them seemed unnaturally loud in that very quiet place.

Although she was jolted Kirsty didn't cry out. She gritted her teeth together against the pain that shot up through her ankle, the same one she had sprained four years ago. Staying in a crouching position close to the ground, she waited, hoping that Neil hadn't heard the rattle of stones when she had fallen.

She hoped in vain. The door opened, and yellow light shafted across the grass, missing her by inches. Neil's figure loomed darkly in the doorway.

'Who's there?' he demanded sharply, and when he didn't get an answer he stepped out and looked around the garden. He saw her and came towards her. Quickly he crouched before her. 'Kirsty!' Surprise lilted through his voice. 'What the hell are you doing here?'

'I saw the light from the other side. I thought someone might have broken into the cottage, so I came to look. I tripped over and fell.' She began to get to her feet. Neil straightened up too.

'Why did you think someone might have broken in?' he asked.

'I knew you'd gone away,' she replied. Tentatively she put her left foot to the ground. Pain shot through her ankle and she couldn't help gasping. 'Oh, dear,' she muttered. Faintness came over her and she swayed. 'I think I've hurt my ankle again.'

'Then you'd better come in and let me look at it ... *again*,' he said dryly, and moving to her side put an arm about her waist.

'No, it's all right. It'll be all right,' She began to limp towards the opening in the wall. 'I'll go home now. Goodnight,'

'Kirsty, stop being so bloody stubborn,' he growled taking hold of her arm. 'You know damn well you can't walk back to the Lodge. I'll drive you there. But first come inside for a few moments, catch your breath.'

His mood wasn't of the best, she could tell by the abrasive note in his voice. Maybe it hadn't worked out with Camille the way he had hoped and that was why he had come back. Perhaps the flighty French girl had hurt his feelings, had found that he was not to her liking after all, had left him and skipped back to Paris.

'No, I. . . .' she began, and put her left foot to the ground again. The pain was worse. Everything whirled about her. Her arms went out in-

stinctively towards him to hold on to him as the
only substantial support she could find and she
fainted.

The faint didn't last long. She came to as Neil
was carrying her through the doorway into the
living room of the cottage.

'I'm sorry,' she mumbled into the soft Shetland
wool of his sweater. 'I've never fainted before. I
didn't mean to. I . . . what I'm trying to say is
that I didn't faint deliberately.'

'No one ever does,' he remarked as he set her
down in the big ladderbacked chair by the hearth.
He pushed her back against the cushion which
was tied to the rungs and looked down at her with
narrowed assessing eyes. 'I'll get you a drink of
water,' he said curtly. 'Then I'll look at your
ankle.'

'Neil, I don't want you to think I fainted just
so you would bring me in here,' she said urgently,
leaning towards him.

'But I don't think that,' he retorted. 'You
fainted because the pain in your ankle got to you.
It's not unusual. Now sit back and relax, I'll be
back in a minute.'

He stepped through an open doorway at the
back of the room into the small kitchenette.
Kirsty leaned back with a sigh and looked
around the room. It hadn't changed much in
four years. The furniture was the same simple
and sturdy, the floor was still covered by woven,
brightly coloured rugs. The same books stood
on the bookshelves by the hearth. The only different things were the curtains at the window

and the electric light. Hamish Taggart had looked after the cottage well in the absence of its owner and it had been let each summer, until now, to families who liked to take a holiday in a Highland croft.

'Here you are,' Neil handed her a glass of water. Hooking a foot under a small three-legged stool, he dragged it over and sat down on it in front of her. 'Now for your boot. This will probably hurt, Kirsty. Ready?'

She nodded. She set the glass of water down on the high stone curb of the hearth and gripped the arms of the chair. Holding the heel and toe of her wellington boot, Neil slowly eased it from her foot. There was more pain, but it wasn't sharp and she didn't feel faint again. Next Neil peeled the short sock from her foot and with their heads almost touching they both peered at her ankle. Neil stroked it with his forefinger and Kirsty shuddered, not with pain, but because he had touched her.

He looked up right into her eyes. Their faces were so close they could have kissed easily. His glance drifted down to her mouth and his lips parted. Kirsty drew back to lean against the cushion again and closed her eyes. Her heart was pounding and her throat felt dry.

'Feeling faint again?' he mocked, and she opened her eyes quickly. He was still sitting before her, his elbows on his knees, his chin in his hands, and was watching her sardonically, the lines from his nostrils to the corners of his mouth very pronounced, his eyes half-closed.

She nodded again and reaching for the glass of water picked it up and sipped from it.

'The sprain isn't bad,' he said. 'Want me to bandage it for you?'

'No, thank you,' she said quickly. Bandaging would mean him touching her again. 'I'll do it myself when I get home.' She licked her lips, sat up straight and asked coolly, 'Why have you come back?'

His eyebrows tilted and he gave her a glance of amused surprise.

'Why shouldn't I come back? This is my place. I like being here and I intend to stay here for the rest of the summer.' His eyes narrowed again. 'Did you think I'd returned to New York?'

'I didn't know what to think,' she murmured, avoiding his penetrating stare and looking down at the half-full glass in her hands. 'Why did you go away with Camille?' she forced herself to ask.

There was a short tense silence. When he didn't answer Kirsty looked at him. He was still staring at her with narrowed eyes.

'I didn't go away with Camille,' he said at last. 'She went away with me.'

He rose to his feet and went over to the dresser with the willow pattern plates on its shelves. Opening the bottom cupboard, he took out a bottle and two glasses. He picked them up and came back to sit on the stool, handing her one of the glasses. 'Here, this might help you to relax a bit,' he said. 'Thaw you out.'

'I'm not cold,' she retorted, but took the glass from him and placed the glass of water back on the hearth curb.

'You may not feel cold, but your attitude is, to say the least ... frigid,' he replied nastily, and drank half his whisky.

'That's because I'm not young and innocent or easily deceived and seduced any more by a man experienced in romancing women,' she retaliated forcefully. 'I'm not like Camille.'

'You can say that again,' he jibed, his eyes blazing with anger, and tossed off the rest of his whisky. He stood up again, stalked over to the dresser and sloshed more whisky into his glass. He didn't come back to the stool but leaned his hips against the dresser. Above the glass as he raised it to his lips his eyes glittered at her, hard and bright. 'Camille had more *savoir-faire* than you ever had or ever will have. She knows what to do to get what she wants. You've never known what it is you want and you've no idea how to get it.'

'Oh.' Kirsty put the glass of whisky which she had hardly tasted down beside the glass of water and with her hands on the arms of the chair she pushed herself upright to stand up, the bare toes of her injured foot resting only lightly on the floor. 'If you're going to be rude I'm leaving,' she retorted furiously.

'You'll have to put your boot on first,' Neil said practically, setting down his glass and coming back to her. 'And to do that you'll have to sit down again.' She didn't move but glared at him defiantly. Standing close to her with his hands on his hips he leaned towards her. 'Sit down, Kirsty. You're not going anywhere. You're staying here.'

'No, I'm not—I'm going home. Oh, what are you doing? Neil Dysart, bring that boot and sock back here at once!' she demanded.

He had picked up her footwear and had gone over to the door. He opened the door and threw the boot and the sock outside. Then he shut the door, turned the key in the lock and pushed the two bolts home. He took the key out of the lock and put it in a blue and white jug on the top shelf of the dresser, then turned to her, his eyes dancing with devilry.

'We're behind a locked door again, Kirsty,' he drawled mockingly.

'You're drunk,' she accused, giving him a scornful glance.

'On two whiskies? Hardly. A little less inhibited than usual, perhaps, but not drunk.' He came back to her and putting a hand against her shoulder he pushed. Kirsty lost her balance and sat down. Immediately Neil sat on the stool, shifting it closer. Resting his arms across her knees, he leaned forward and looked into her eyes. 'When you're angry they change colour,' he whispered. 'They become a deep, almost purple blue, the colour of the loch on a fine day, and looking into them I feel I could drown willingly in them.'

'Stop it, stop it,' she whispered. She put her hands against her cheeks and shook her head. 'Oh, I don't know how you can do it!'

'Do what?' he queried, leaning closer, his breath feathering her lips.

'Try to make love to me when you've been with her.'

'With whom?'

'With Camille.'

'I haven't been with Camille.'

'Yes, you have.' She sat back in the chair as far away as possible. 'You said yourself she went away with you. And in the note she left for Hussein she said she'd gone with you.'

'Did she?' His eyebrows tilted derisively. 'And how did his Excellency react to that?'

'He was very upset. You see, he'd invited her here with her parents so he could propose marriage to her.'

'I know. Camille told me.'

'You knew? Then why did you take her away with you?' she exclaimed. 'Oh, you're even more despicable than I'd believed!'

'Am I?' His eyes glinted dangerously. 'What makes you say that?'

'You must have known, too, that Hussein couldn't ask her to marry him once she'd been with another man.'

'Now, hold on,' he rebuked her sharply. 'Just what do you mean by her having been with another man?'

'She went away with you somewhere yesterday and . . . and . . . well, you and she stayed the night together,' she said uncertainly.

'That's what I thought you meant,' he said, his lips thinning.

'And before she went away with you you did all you could to entice her away. You took her to a dance in the village. You met her in secret and then you eloped with her.'

'I admit to taking her to the village dance,' he retorted. 'I was sorry for her that evening at dinner.' She'd told me she was fed up with staying at the Lodge. She also told me she was sick and tired of waiting for Hussein to propose and seeing him making eyes at you and hanging on every word you said to him.' His upper lip lifted in a sneer and his glance raked her. 'I felt a bit sick myself watching him make up to you and seeing you lap up the attention he gave you. Everyone noticed how besotted he was with you and how you were encouraging him.'

'I did not encourage Hussein!' she flared.

'No?' Neil laughed jeeringly. 'Yet you told me yourself you might marry him . . . for his money.'

'But that was before I knew he was thinking of marrying Camille,' she retorted. 'Once I knew that he was thinking of marrying her I put the idea right out of my head. And I could never do what you did. I could never stoop to do what you did, knowing what you did. Oh, Neil, why did you elope with her? And where is she now? What have you done with her?'

He drew his breath in with a sharp hissing noise as if he had reached the end of his patience.

'More than any other woman I know you have the ability to enrage me,' he said between taut lips. 'Firstly I did not *elope* with Camille. All I did was drive her to Glasgow.'

'Why?'

'When she knew I was going there yesterday she asked me if she could go with me because she wanted to fly to London from there. She said she couldn't stand staying at Balmore any longer and would I help her get away. I agreed because, as I've said, I was sorry for her. I dropped her off in the city where I knew she could get a bus to the airport. I haven't seen her since.'

'Then you didn't stay the night with her,' she mumbled.

'I didn't stay the night with her,' he repeated slowly and with mocking emphasis on every word. 'I've never been particularly attracted to blondes and I found her juvenile chatter about the great time she's going to have once she's the wife of Sheikh al Dukar extremely irritating. She's determined to marry Hussein, you know.'

'No, I don't know. If she's so keen to marry him she shouldn't have gone away with you.'

'She was hoping to draw his attention away from you and back to her, can't you see that? And she told me she intended to phone her parents as soon as she got to London to let them know where she was. Did she?'

'Someone phoned them,' she replied. While he had been explaining he had drawn back from her and she used the opportunity to rise to her feet again. At once he sprang to his feet.

'Where are you going?' he demanded.

'Back to Balmore . . . if you would kindly unlock the door and let me have my sock and boot,' she said tartly.

'Is the Sheikh still there?'

'No. He left this morning to go and look for Camille. He's not coming back,' she replied woodenly.

'Are you sure he isn't?'

'Quite sure. Thanks to Camille and to you I've lost a good tenant and a potential buyer for Balmore.'

'Good. I'm glad. It was worth behaving despicably with Camille, as you call it, to get rid of him.'

'You mean you. . . .' Kirsty broke off to stare at him. Mischief and mockery sparkled in his eyes. 'Oh, you've done nothing else but cause trouble since you came back!' she seethed. 'First you rescued the poachers, then you encouraged Camille to run away, to say nothing of how you made me appear to Hussein's uncle by keeping me with you behind a locked door in the turret for an hour.'

'You can blame Ahmed for that,' he replied. 'He did the tale-telling to his boss.'

'But you did ask me to go up to the turret room with you.'

'Only because I wanted to make love to you,' he said softly, coming closer to her and putting his hands on her shoulders. 'As I do now.'

'No, I don't want you to. I. . . .'

His lips covered hers, smothering the rest of what she had been going to say. His arms went around her to prevent her from escaping. She tried not to respond, but the movement of his lips against hers was both seductive and forceful. Her lips parted and her body went slack against his.

Briefly he lifted his lips from hers so he could whisper tauntingly.

'Do you still dare to say you don't want to make

love with me? Your lips and your body are telling me a different story.

Thick lashes shadowed his eyes and his lips curved into the tender loving smile she had come to know so well in this same room four years ago. Her heart leapt in response and as he loosened her hair from its topknot so that it swirled down about her shoulders he kissed her again, a demanding, bruising kiss that made her head whirl. All her misgivings were swept away by the passion which flooded through her in response to that kiss. Her arms went around him, her fingers caressed his neck and tangled in his hair. It was as if they had never been parted; as if the past four years had never been.

'Kirsty, stay here tonight. Sleep with me.'

His voice was deep and a little shaken as his lips moved among the silky fragrance of her hair where it lay against her temple and his arms still held her closely. Through his clothing and hers she could feel the thrust and throb of his desire.

But his words shocked her back to the reality of the situation. Four years ago when he had made the same suggestion she had agreed willingly. Now everything was different. The abrupt manner of his leaving, his silence for four years had changed her from an impulsive girl, willing to give herself in love, into a cautious woman determined to protect herself from hurt.

She tried to pull free of him, but his hands slid down to her waist and tightened. They seemed to her to be unbelievably strong. So did he. He was a strong, ruthless man who was determined to take what he wanted.

'I can't,' she whispered. 'I can't stay the night with you, nor sleep with you.'

'Why not?' Laughter lilted in his voice and he tried to draw her towards him, but she remained stiff and unyielding. 'I know you want to stay as much as I want you to stay,' he continued softly and coaxingly. 'We've been apart for so long, let other people come between us, but now we're together again all the old hungers have awakened.' He managed to pull her closer, his arms sliding around her in a warm embrace, and pressed his cheek against her head. 'I ache for you, Kirsty,' he whispered. 'Deep inside I hurt for you, ever since we met over a week ago on the cliff above the big pool. God knows when I came back to Balmore I didn't expect this to happen to me . . . to us . . . but it has, and I'm going to ask you again. Please stay here, tonight.'

'No, no, I can't!' Fear of her own responses gave her the strength to resist. She twisted free of his embrace and limped towards the door.

'I could easily make you stay,' he threatened, moving after her.

'I doubt it would give you much pleasure if you did, if you made me stay and sleep with you against my will,' she retorted coolly, her head up, her eyes returning his challenging gaze steadily. She knew only too well how easy he would find persuading her to stay once he touched her again. 'Please, Neil, don't shame yourself or me by doing something we'll both regret later,' she continued. 'Please accept my refusal. I can't stay with you. I . . . I don't trust you.'

He was jolted, she could see. His head jerked back as if she had hit him again. For a moment empathy with his pain tempted her to relent, to take back what she had said, to fling her arms about him and offer herself and her love to him unconditionally, regardless of consequences. But she kept thinking of his wife, and she knew that if she gave into her own passionate desires to stay the night with him she would never be able to live with herself comfortably again.

'I'd like to go home now,' she said, turning away and going towards the door. The need to be alone with her misery was becoming overwhelming. She had to get away from him before she broke down and wept for the love they had once known and might have known again if she could have changed her values.

'All right.' He spoke coldly and a little wearily. Behind her Kirsty heard him move to the dresser, take down the jug where he had put the key. Soon he was unbolting and unlocking the door. He stepped outside and returned with her boot and sock. While she put them on he went out again to start his car.

They sat side by side in the front of the Jaguar. Sitting bolt upright and staring straight ahead, Kirsty watched the pale moonlit trunks of trees flit by as the car went along the lochside road. The silence was heavy with unspoken thoughts and feelings. It was so different from the time Neil had driven her back to the Lodge the night they had first met; when he had kept stopping the car at the roadside to turn to her and take her in his arms; when a ten-minute drive had taken over an hour.

Outside the factor's house he said politely without looking at her.

'Would you like me to help you into the house?'

'No, thank you. I can manage.' She opened the door and stepped out, careful not to put weight on her right foot. She glanced inside the car before she closed the door. 'Thank you for bringing me home,' she said.

She slammed the door closed and limped towards the house as fast as she could. Behind her the car reversed and left the courtyard swiftly, with a squeal of tyres. High up in the dark blue, star-pricked sky the full moon seemed to grin mockingly.

CHAPTER SEVEN

PEARL grey mist was peeling back from the waters of Loch Linnhe, the long sea-loch which delves almost into the middle of the Highlands, when Kirsty drove into Fort William next morning.

For her the night had been long and tormented by the demons of churned-up emotions and physical yearnings, and she had been glad when daybreak had come so that she could get ready to visit Dawson, Pettigrew and Tanner. She had dressed in a suit made from fine burgundy-coloured wool and with it she wore a white silk blouse frilled at the neckline, its soft femininity contrasting with the severe tailoring of the suit.

In Fort William she parked the car near the pier and walked back to the main street to the tall white buildings where the lawyer's offices were located.

'Thank you for coming here today, Lady Whyte,' said Douglas Pettigrew, after she had been shown into his room by a secretary. He was a fresh-faced, red-haired man of about thirty-five or six and he looked as if he would have been much more at home on the farm driving a tractor than sitting behind a desk. 'Please sit down.' He brought a chair forward, then went round to the other side of the desk to wait until Kirsty had sat down before taking his seat in a black leather swivel chair.

He leaned forward, placed his arms on the desk and clasped his hands together. His grey eyes stared at her intently.

'To tell the truth I'm not sure where to begin,' he admitted. 'The whole business is so complicated.'

'I really don't understand why you have to discuss my late husband's will with me,' said Kirsty coolly. 'It's before probate at the moment and seemed to be taking a long time to be approved.'

'Probate does take a long time,' he replied. 'Especially if there is some doubt about the will's legality.' He looked down at the desk, frowned, then looked at her again. 'Lady Whyte, you're not going to like what I have to tell you, but I can think of no other way than to put it bluntly.'

'Then please be blunt,' she replied with a slight impish grin. 'I'm really quite tough, you know.'

'Well, here goes. Sir Alec Whyte had no right to leave Balmore to you, because he was never the owner of the estate,' he said.

'But . . . but his father, Sir Ian Whyte, left it to Alec in his will,' exclaimed Kirsty, here eyes opening wide.

'No, he didn't. Sir Ian only left the estate to Sir Alec *in trust*. That means that Alec was allowed to live there and look after the estate while he was alive. Once Sir Alec died the property was to pass to Sir Ian's younger son, Mr Neil Dysart-Whyte, who would also assume the title.'

Kirsty didn't move, but it seemed to her that all sorts of strange sounds twanged and sizzled in her head.

'Go on, please,' she said rather weakly.

'You've heard of Mr Dysart-Whyte, perhaps?' he queried.

'I know a Neil Dysart. He's a surgeon and he's the tenant of a croft on the estate. I know, also, that he is Sir Ian Whyte's illegitimate son,' she said stiffly.

'Er, yes. Just so. Well now.' Douglas Pettigrew rubbed his jaw, and the bristles of his beard rustled. He shuffled some papers on his desk, found the one he wanted and leaning back in his chair studied it.

'It is true that Mr Dysart-Whyte was born out of wedlock,' he announced. 'However, just before he died Sir Ian married Morag Dysart and had the birth of their son legitimtised.'

'Oh. Can that be done?' exclaimed Kirsty.

'It can be done and was done. My father, who was legal adviser to Sir Ian, arranged it, and here is the proof.' He leaned across the desk to hand her the paper. She took it.

'Then why doesn't Neil Dysart use the name Whyte?' she asked.

'You would have to ask him that yourself,' he replied. 'I would suspect that by the time he could use it legally he was already established in his profession as a surgeon and preferred to continue to use the name he was known by. He told me the other day when he was here that he didn't know he was Sir Ian's son until four years ago. His mother told him just before she died.'

'Neil was here, the other day?' Kirsty gasped.

'Yes. You see. . . .' Douglas Pettigrew broke off

and sighed. 'But I'm jumping ahead of myself. To go back to Sir Ian. After he had legitimatised his second son's birth he made his will.' He picked up another document. 'This is it.' He handed it over to her. 'If you read it you will see very clearly that he left the estate of Balmore *in trust* only to his *adopted* son Alec William Whyte for as long as he lived. On Alec's death the title and the property would be passed on, as usual in the Whyte family, to his own eldest son, Neil Allan Dysart-Whyte, to whom he would have willed everything directly if Sir Alec had not existed.'

Kirsty stared down at the printed words in front of her, searching for the word *adopted*. It wasn't hard to find because it had been underlined.

'I didn't know Sir Alec had been adopted. He didn't tell me,' she murmured, putting the document down on the desk.

'Apparently Sir Ian's first wife, Constance, tried several times to have a child but miscarried. So a baby was adopted,' explained the lawyer. 'We have the adoption papers here. Again my father was the lawyer involved.' Documents rustled as he handed them to her.

Kirsty studied them, her brain seeming to burst with bewilderment.

'But if your father was Sir Ian's legal adviser why did he let my husband, Sir Alec, make a will leaving the estate to me?' she asked at last.

'He was not consulted by Sir Alec on the matter of a will or on anything else legal,' said Douglas Pettigrew dryly. 'After Sir Ian's death

Sir Alec broke all connection with this firm, turned all his business over to a firm of lawyers in Glasgow.' His lips turned a downward curve. 'It seems that Sir Alec did not like anyone to remind him that he had been adopted or that Balmore was not legally his, and he knew that my father would never agree to draw up a will leaving the property to you because my father knew about the other will.'

'Then why haven't you told me before now?' demanded Kirsty. 'Why have you taken so long, nearly five months, to inform me?'

'We wanted to find Mr Neil Dysart-Whyte first.' Douglas Pettigrew had the grace to look embarrassed. 'We had to make sure he was alive. It took a while for our letter to reach him. You see, he had moved away from New York and hadn't told Sir Alec of his whereabouts. When he didn't reply immediately we were thinking of writing to him again, but fortunately he arrived here three weeks ago. He had come in answer to our letter, he said, and he was very surprised by what we had to tell him. He had no idea that his father had named him to be heir to the estate after the death of Sir Alec.'

'So what should I do now?' Kirsty was aware of a lightness, as if a burden had been lifted suddenly from her shoulders. She was no longer responsible for Balmore. She didn't have to worry any more about letting it to a tenant or selling it. It wasn't hers to worry about. It was Neil's.

'Now, that is exactly why I asked you to come and see me,' said Mr Pettigrew. 'As the executor of of Sir Ian's will my father has the right to contest the validity of Sir Alec's will before the probate court. Naturally we have consulted with Mr Dysart-Whyte and asked him if he wished to contest Sir Alec's will. He said he would think about it and let us know. In the meantime we thought we should get in touch with you and ask you if you want to go ahead and try to have Sir Alec's will proved.'

'Do I have to give you an answer straight away?' asked Kirsty.

'No, of course not. I realise this must be something of a shock to you and that you must have time to consider the situation. I believe you've let the estate for six months to a tenant.'

'Oh, he's left and he won't be coming back.' Kirsty chewed at her lower lip. 'If . . . if I decide to withdraw Sir Alec's will and Mr Dysart inherits the estate does he become responsible for the mortgage?'

'He does. It isn't a personal debt. You are responsible as Sir Alec's wife only for his personal debts. Perhaps I should also warn you that if you don't withdraw Sir Alec's will you could become involved in an expensive and lengthy lawsuit.' Douglas Pettigrew rose to his feet and Kirsty stood up too, realising that the interview was at an end because he had other clients to see.

'Thank you for your advice,' she said. 'I . . . I'll let you know soon, probably tomorrow, what I'm going to do.'

'Don't be too hasty now,' he said pleasantly, opening the door for her. 'Good morning, Lady Whyte.'

Kirsty walked back to the pier. Sunlight dazzled the water of the loch. Seagulls and terns soared and glided above the few fishing boats which had tied up. Two touring buses had arrived and their passengers, mostly elderly men and women, exchanged jokes and remarks as they gathered together in friendly groups before setting off to explore the old town.

A longing to take off on holiday, to drive away, far away from Balmore and its problems, surged through Kirsty as she unlocked the door of the car. She could do that now. Instead of going north she could drive south, go to Edinburgh to see Duncan and his family, go to Glasgow to see her parents. She could go and never come back, start a new life for herself. She was free, a liberated woman, bound to no one but herself.

But she was also bound to her own emotions and her own sense of values, she thought with a sigh, as she slid behind the steering wheel. She couldn't leave Balmore yet. She couldn't leave until she had decided to relinquish her claim to the estate by withdrawing Alec's will from probate. She couldn't leave until she had seen Neil again and had asked him why he hadn't told her he knew about his father's will.

She started the car and drove back to the main street, automatically turning left and taking the road north. Now that she knew about Sir Ian's will she could make sense of Neil's behaviour the day they had met on the bluff above the big pool. She could understand now why he hadn't liked the idea of Balmore being sold to Hussein.

Then why hadn't he told her he knew Balmore was his? And why hadn't Alec told her Balmore wasn't his? All the way back to the Lodge she tussled with the conundrum, and was no closer to having solved it when she reached the parting of the ways where the road turned to curve round the head of the loch or sloped up the hill to the big house. Stopping the car, she looked over at Cairn Rua. Purple and brown, splashed with patches of bright green, its rocky red summit glowing in the sunlight, it looked inviting, a good place to spend a summer's afternoon, walking and perhaps lazing in the depths of the heather.

On impulse Kirsty drove beside the loch. She would go and see Neil again and have it out with him, once and for all. The small car had trouble getting up the steep hill to the cottage, but eventually she was there, and she stopped it on the level sward of grass.

The cottage door was closed. No one sat in front of it on an old deckchair and the Jaguar wasn't parked beside the house. Neil wasn't there.

At the Lodge she went straight to the big kitchen where she knew Hamish would be having his midday meal with Mary.

'Any dinner for me, Mary?' she asked when she walked in.

'Aye, if you like mince and tatties, there is,' replied the housekeeper, getting to her feet and going over to the cooker. 'Sit yourself down.'

'I was over at the croft on Cairn Rua, looking for Neil Dysart,' Kirsty said to Hamish. 'Have you seen him lately?'

'Aye—this morning. He's away to Skye for a few days, to do some rock climbing in the Cuillins. He says he'll be back on Friday,' replied Hamish in his slow way.

'Oh, I see. Thank you.' Kirsty forced herself to smile as Mary set a plate of vegetables in front of her.

She ate in silence, thinking about Neil. He hadn't hesitated to go away for a change of scene. He hadn't let his emotions or his sense of values come between him and doing what he wanted to do. But then he never had. What he wanted had always come first with him. And if he couldn't get what he wanted, as he hadn't been able to last night when he had wanted her, he just turned his back and went away.

'I'll be in Sir Alec's bedroom this afternoon, if you need me for anything,' she announced as she finished eating and laid her knife and fork down on the plate. 'There's a box of his papers in there that I've been intending to go through before I go away.'

Both Mary and Hamish looked up sharply— the first time either of them had ever reacted quickly to anything she had ever said, she thought sardonically.

'Did you say you're going away?' said Mary.

'Yes. I've decided to have a wee holiday.'

'Och, now I'm thinking that's a good idea, so it is,' said Mary, nodding. 'How long will you be gone?'

'I'm not sure. I'll write to you and tell you when to expect me back. I'll be leaving early in the

morning. I'll arrange for all the mail to be delivered to a lawyer's office in Fort William while
I'm away. A Mr Douglas Pettigrew will look after
all the business to do with the estate.' Kirsty
noticed Hamish and Mary exchange knowing
glances and knew they had recognised the name
Pettigrew. 'All right?' she said enquiringly.

'Aye, that's fine, just fine,' murmured Hamish,
and got on with the process of lighting his pipe.

Alec's bedroom was on the ground floor next
to the study. It wasn't very big and Kirsty knew
that at one time it had been a room where breakfast had been served. Since it faced east it received
none of the afternoon sunshine and with its plain
dark furniture and curtains it seemed drab and
dull that day.

The box where he had stored his personal letters was in the bottom of the wardrobe. It was
about four feet long, two feet wide and about a
foot deep. It was made from teak and had an
intricate design carved on its lid. It was heavy
and Kirsty had a struggle to lift it out. The key
was on a ring on which Alec had also kept the
keys to his desk and filing cabinets and which he
had kept on his person at all times. Now that ring
was in one of the drawers of the desk, so she went
into the study to get it.

The box opened easily and her eyes widened
with surprise when she saw it was full of books,
all of them bound in black and all of them the
same size. Picking up one of them, she found the
date of a year printed on it in gold letters and
underneath the date the words, Daily Journal. She

opened the book and flicked over pages. Most of them were filled with Alec's rather crabbed writing. The books were his diaries which he had kept, judging by the dates on them, for nearly forty years, from the year in which he had turned nineteen until a year before his death when the creeping paralysis had taken away the strength from his hands and had made it impossible for him to write.

Kirsty took all the books out of the box, hoping to find letters stored underneath them. But there were only a few letters, and not one of them was the one she was looking for. She put them back and began to place the diaries on top of them one by one, glancing through each briefly, discovering as she did Alec's bitterness and unhappiness when Morag Dysart had showed her preference for his father; his obsessive love for Balmore and his bitter hatred of Neil.

Skipping over several years, she looked for and found the diary for the year she had first come to work for Alec and read about his reaction to her. She flicked over pages to the day Neil had left Balmore.

'Neil Dysart had the nerve to come and see me again today. He wanted to see Christina to tell her he has to go to New York. It seems he has a chance to work with a great American orthopaedic surgeon. I saw an opportunity to be rid of him. I encouraged him to go. He insisted stubbornly on seeing Christina. He said he wanted to ask her to marry him, and I lied to him. I told him how fickle she is. He was upset but still steadfast. I told him she is going to marry me, but he didn't believe me. He asked if he could leave a letter for her, and I agreed. After he had gone I opened the letter. There was a proposal of marriage in it. I burned it.'

Kirsty turned the page and read his account of his discussion with her about Neil.

'I had to lie to Christina too. I told her Neil is like his father, lacking in morals where women are concerned. She took it well. I admire her. She's clever too—she could help me restore Balmore. When she's got over Neil I'll ask her to marry her. If only I could raise some money. The annuity Father left me is not enough to do what I want to do. If only he hadn't been so damned extravagant.'

Kirsty closed the diary and sat for a while on the edge of the bed thinking about Alec and how with a few words he had been able to destroy her trust in Neil and Neil's trust in her. She put the diary in the box and picked up the one for the year Alec had made his will. Soon she was reading about that.

'I cannot bear to think of my beloved Balmore being inherited by the son of that womaniser who calls himself my father. Today I have made a will leaving everything to my dear Kirsty. God knows she deserves the place, she has worked so hard to improve it. I've engaged another lawyer to help me draw up the will. Now I hope and pray it will not be contested by that old fool Pettigrew.'

Kirsty returned all the diaries to the box and locked it up. She carried it back to the wardrobe and left the bedroom. Now she knew what to do. She went back to the factor's house and began to make preparations for her departure the next day.

She wrote to Robert Rankin, Alec's lawyer, and asked him to withdraw Alec's will from probate because she had realised, after reading his diaries, that the balance of her late husband's mind had been disturbed when he had made the will, and she told him to contact Douglas Pettigrew for further information. Then she wrote to Douglas Pettigrew telling him what she had done. Then she wrote to Neil, telling him why she had left Balmore. The first two letters she intended to post; the letter to Neil she left on the desk in the factor's office.

She slept well that night and was up early the next day. After breakfast she carried her suitcases out to the car. It was another misty morning with promise of a warm sunny day. As she drove out of the yard she kept her glance on the road, determined not to look at the view of the loch in case she was tempted to stay. She refused to be held back by sentiment any more. The road before her led into the future, her future, and she had chosen to go forward alone.

In Balvaig she stopped at Jessie's house. Her friend was having her breakfast.

'I've decided to take your advice. I'm going away for a holiday,' said Kirsty. 'The trouble is I don't know where to go. I'd thought of visiting Duncan or my parents, but I've deciced I want to be on my own for a while in a place where nobody knows me.'

'My cousin and her husband run a small private hotel in Galloway, near a little fishing village.' Jessie's glance was bright and shrewd. 'I don't suppose you're too flush with funds and their terms are fairly moderate. If you like I could telephone them for you, tell them you're on the way and you're a friend of mine.'

'I'd be glad if you would. How long do you think it will take me to get there?'

'You should be there in time for dinner this evening. I'll get you a map book and show you exactly where it is.'

Later that afternoon Kirsty stopped her car outside the front door of an imposing house built of blocks of grey granite which stood on a hillside above the small village of Kirkford. Getting out of the car, she stretched and looked about her.

Over the slate roofs and chimneypots of the houses below the hill, she could see the estuary of the river. The tide was in and the blue water was ruffled by a breeze. Several small sailing boats all going the same way, the white triangles of their sails taut and shining, heeled over. They were presumably taking part in a race and were aiming for a buoy which she could just see bobbing on the waves where the estuary flowed into the sea.

She looked back at the house. It looked sedate yet well cared for, a quiet place where she could rest and collect her thoughts together. She went up the few steps, opened the vestibule door and stepped into the hallway. On the small reception desk there was a bell. She pressed it and in a few moments a woman a little older than Jessie appeared.

'I'm Kirsty Whyte. My friend Jessie phoned you and reserved a room for me,' said Kirsty.

'I'm pleased to meet you. I'm Maude Finlay,' said the other woman, with a cheerful smile. 'And the room is all ready. It's a good thing Jessie phoned, because it was the last vacant room and we've had lots of enquiries this afternoon. The fine weather has brought people on holiday. Now if you would just be signing the register, I'll take you up to your room. Have you ever been to Galloway before?'

CHAPTER EIGHT

FOUR days later, dressed in her tartan pants and wearing a Fair Isle sweater patterned in green and white, Kirsty strode along the firm white sand of a broad beach. Although the day was sunny the wind was strong and grey clouds scurried before it across a sky of pale blue.

Enjoying the sting of salt spray on her cheeks and the roar and hiss of the waves as they advanced and retreated, she walked right to the end of the beach. It was the last day of her stay in Kirkford. Tomorrow she would have to leave because she couldn't afford to stay any longer. Yet she was still undecided about what to do. Should she return to Balmore? Or should she go to her parents' home in Glasgow and start looking for a job?

When she had walked far enough she returned to the hotel and went up to her room. After washing she changed into the blue dress she had worn so often for social occasions at Balmore, brushed her hair and coiled it neatly, then went downstairs to the dining room for dinner, taking her seat at a small table near the window.

She was studying the menu when a voice she recognised only too well said,

'I'd like to sit here, if the lady doesn't object.'

Kirsty looked up slowly. Above the edge of the menu she saw a jacket made from fine greenish

174

tweed. She looked higher and saw a crisp cream shirt and a dark green tie. Even higher she met the cool glance of amber-brown eyes set between short thick lashes. Above them a lock of reddish-brown hair slid forward across a high forehead.

'Do you mind if I sit here?' Neil asked suavely. 'The waitress would like to know.'

Kirsty glanced at the waitress, who was staring at her curiously.

'No, not at all.' She made an effort to appear as suave and cool as he was. 'Please sit down.'

He sat opposite to her, the waitress offered him a menu and departed.

'I found out where you were staying from your friend Jessie,' he said in a pleasant conversational tone. 'Mary Taggart suggested she might know where you'd gone for your holiday.' He looked up from the menu and his eyes were coldly critical. 'Why the hell did you run away, Kirsty?' he rapped.

'I didn't run away, I just left. I decided I needed a change like you did. You went to Skye. I came here,' she retorted, and looked down at her menu again.

'But you don't intend to go back to Balmore,' he accused softly. 'Mary says you took everything you own with you. You left nothing behind.'

She was saved from having to reply by the return of the waitress, who had brought knives and forks to set in front of Neil. When his place was set the waitress took their orders and went away again taking the menus with her.

'I did leave something behind,' said Kirsty. 'I

left a letter for you. Did you get it?'

'I did. That's why I'm here.'

'You should have told me why you'd come back to Scotland, or you should have let Mr Pettigrew tell me,' she said. 'You should have told me about your father's will. Why didn't you?'

Neil picked up a fork and began to make patterns on the tablecloth with the prongs, his eyes hidden by their lashes, his mouth twisting slightly.

'I hoped you and I could work something out, a way of sharing the place between us. I didn't want to take it from you, or fight with you over it,' he told her. 'I was stalling for time by not telling you, time in which I could get to know you again.' His mouth tightened and he flicked a glance across the table at her. 'I gave Pettigrew hell for telling you about my father's will. I was going to tell you myself when we'd sorted out this other more personal matter.'

'What other more personal matter?' she whispered.

'You know what I mean,' he retorted. 'We've fallen in love again with each other.'

'No, we haven't. We're not in love.' She got to her feet. 'Please tell the waitress I've changed my mind and I don't want anything to eat,' she muttered, and hurried away quickly, leaving the room before Neil had risen to his feet.

She sped up the stairs to her room. Taking out the suitcase she had brought up to the room when she had moved in, she began to pack it, throwing the clothes into it anyhow. The case was half full when the doorknob turned, and she looked round, wishing she had thought to lock the door. The door opened and Neil stepped into the room. He closed the door and leaned against it.

'That wasn't a very clever move on your part,' he remarked dryly.

'Oh, please go away and leave me alone,' Kirsty replied shakily, and continued to stuff clothes into the case.

'No. I'm not leaving you alone until you agree to marry me.' he replied.

'Marry you?' she gasped, staring at him. 'How can I marry you when you're married already.'

'I'm not married,' he retorted.

'Yes, you are. Alec told me you married Barbara Gow, the heiress, three years ago.'

'I used to be married to Barbara. But I'm not married to her now and haven't been married to her for over a year. She and I split after twelve months of marriage. She found she didn't like being married to a surgeon who was dedicated to his work and who didn't have time to dance attendance on her all the time.' His voice rasped with bitterness. 'So she left me, and I wasn't a bit sorry when she did.'

'Oh!' Kirsty's legs felt suddenly shaky and she slumped down on the edge of the bed. 'I didn't know. I . . . I'm sorry.'

'About what?'

Neil lunged away from the door and came over to the bed. Lifting the half-full suitcase off the bed, he put it on the floor and sat down beside her. Every nerve quivering in response to his nearness Kirsty kept her glance on the case on the floor.

'I'm sorry your marriage broke up,' she muttered.

'You don't have to be sorry. Barbara and I married for all the wrong reasons. She wanted a man who would be her escort, who would be content to walk in her shadow. And I . . . .' He broke off, and Kirsty looked at him. He was also staring at her case, his face set in grim lines.

'And you?' she prompted, and he twisted on the bed to face her.

'I married her on the rebound from being in love with you,' he said harshly. 'When I didn't get an answer to the letter I left for you I came to the conclusion that you were everything Alec had said you were.' He laughed shortly when she looked away, shaking her head. 'You still don't believe me, do you? You don't believe I was so deeply in love with you my world turned upside down when you didn't answer my letter. To your way of thinking men aren't supposed to have feelings that can be hurt.'

There was a short silence. Evening sunlight poured into the bedroom through the window, gilding everything. Outside a thrush warbled its last song of the day.

'Barbara had hurt her leg in a skiing accident, and Weingarten let me operate on it,' Neil said more quietly. 'The operation was successful. Her gratitude was overwhelming.' He laughed again, shortly, in self-derision. 'She made love to me, proposed marriage to me. She was wealthy, an heiress, well known, and I knew it would further my career if I married a New York socialite. The attendant publicity would help me make it to the top in my profession.' He drew in his breath. 'We deserved to break up. There was nothing deep in our relationship. We didn't really care about each other; we were just dazzled by each other's outward show. She was attracted by the glamour surrounding a young surgeon who had saved her leg. I was . . . well, I've told you I was in a hell of a mess emotionally speaking and had decided to put fame and fortune before anything else.' There was another silence then he added softly, 'You are going to marry me, aren't you now that you know I'm free to marry you?'

'I don't know. I'm not sure that I can,' she muttered.

'So you're still not trusting me. You still believe what Alec told you about me,' he said, his voice low and bitter. 'Yet I've never asked any other woman to marry me, Kirsty. I've never wanted to share my life with any woman the way I'd like to share it with you. I asked you to marry me four years ago in a letter. If you'd received it and had accepted my proposal we'd be married now. We might have had a child. Oh God, Kirsty, when I think of the time we could have been together and haven't been together, all because Alec didn't give you my letter, I feel murderous towards him!'

His voice grated and his hands clenched on his knees. She reached out and laid a hand over one of his, her fingers stroking the tanned skin soothingly.

'Please don't feel like that about Alec. We must both forgive him for what he did,' she whispered. 'I think he must have been mentally unbalanced and very jealous of you. He burned your letter.'

His hand turned under hers and opened to grasp her fingers tightly before she could withdraw them.

'How do you know?' he demanded hoarsely.

'I found his diaries and read parts of them. They're in a box in his bedroom at the Lodge. If I'd only opened the box when he died and had read them then I'd have known he was never the owner of Balmore and so he couldn't leave it to me in his will. And I'd have known you were telling the truth about your letter,' she explained.

'He wrote it all down?' Neil exclaimed. 'Why?'

'I think he was always a very lonely person, not given to confiding in other people, so he confided in a diary. Writing down what he had done was like making a confession and perhaps eased the guilt he felt about wanting to be revenged on your father and mother for making him suffer. Your mother was right. He did hate you, because you were the product of your mother's love for your father. He lied to you about me because he wanted to hurt you and he lied to me about you, not because he wanted to hurt me but because he wanted to hurt you again through me.'

'And he did. He did,' he sighed.

'He also hated you because you were the real son of Sir Ian and would one day possess Balmore.' Kirsty's voice faltered slightly. 'That's why he made a will leaving it to me. He loved

Balmore more than any person. It was his obsession.'

'I had no idea that he'd been in love with my mother,' Neil said. 'No idea at all. It explains a lot.'

'I didn't know until Mary told me. He met your mother when he was a student in Edinburgh, and took her home. She met your father and never looked at Alec again. He was terribly hurt, and soon afterwards the disease began to show itself. In his diary he admitted that he contemplated suicide at that time. I think it was then he transferred his affection from people to plants and animals, to the estate.'

'You seem to have understood him. Did you love him?'

'I did, but not in the way you mean. I admired him and I enjoyed working with him. But I never felt comfortable with him, I never wanted to put my arms around him or to rest my head against his shoulder. I never wanted to sleep with him,' she added, looking down at their clasped hands.

'Poor Alec,' Neil said softly. 'You're right—we must forgive him, even though he hurt both of us.' His glance was slightly mocking as it met hers. 'But maybe I'm presuming too much. Maybe you weren't hurt.'

'Oh, I was. I was! I was miserable for weeks, for months after you'd gone away. And it's been hard to forgive you, to start trusting you again. Knowing you were married didn't help.'

'But I wasn't married, and I'm not married now. I started to tell you in the turret room that you were on the wrong track, but you wouldn't stop to listen.'

'You didn't try to tell me the other night at the cottage,' she reminded him tartly, trying to pull her hand free and failing. The strong surgeon's fingers gripped hers masterfully.

'I'd forgotten that you didn't know,' he replied. 'Do you mean to say you refused to stay the night with me because you believed I was still married to Barbara?' he said tautly. 'Was that why you said you didn't trust me?'

Sensing that he was angry, she tried to free her hand again and shifted away from him along the bed as she nodded.

'Then why the hell didn't you say so?' he thundered, coming after her.

'I don't know, I don't know,' she babbled. 'Oh, Neil, don't be angry with me. I've been so confused since you came back, wanting to love you, wanting to be with you yet not daring to in case it led to disaster.'

'If you'd asked me I could have told you I wasn't married, couldn't I?' he said, his eyes glinting dangerously. 'You know, I could punish you for not asking me. I spent one of the most miserable nights of my life because you refused to stay with me.'

'You don't have to punish me. I've been punished already. I went through hell that night too,' Kirsty said. He had released her hand and had moved away from her, and his sudden withdrawal bothered her. 'How would you punish me?' she asked curiously.

'By walking o... Neil, flicking a ... should I bother to s... know what she wan... love? In fact, I'm be... came after you. Hell!' ... his hair and leaned forwa... his knees and his head betw... be going crazy, behaving as ... early twenties instead of in my m... running after a woman who's rejected m... within the space of two weeks and who's probably going to reject me again if I try to kiss her.' He pushed back his sleeve to look at his watch. 'Seven-thirty. Any idea what time they finish serving dinner here?'

'No.'

Kirsty edged along the bed closer to him. Putting out a hand she touched his shoulder. Her fingers spread along the smooth fine tweed of his jacket to the nape of his neck and twined in the thickness of his hair.

'I'm glad you followed me,' she said softly.

Neil turned his head slowly to look at her. She watched his glance slant down to her mouth. Then she was watching his mouth too, seeing the lips part as they came nearer. Longing to feel their pressure against hers and to know again the touch of his hands, she lifted her mouth enticingly, parting her lips, and from under her drooping lashes watched his lips come closer, feeling long dormant nerves quiver alive in anticipation of being excited by his touch.

here, glad you've come,' she
ase don't go away from me again.'
g the urgings of passion at last, she
d the knot of his tie and began to flick
ndone the buttons of his shirt. Her eager hands
pushed open the shirt and her fingers slid greedily
over the hairy warmth of his chest, pressing and
pinching until she heard his sharp intake of
breath. With a sigh she rested her head against
him. Under her ear his heart changed beat.

'How strongly your heart beats, strong man,'
she whispered. 'And your skin is like velvet. Oh,
Neil, I've wanted to do this for a long, long time!'

'At last you admit it.' He spoke thickly, his arms
going around her, tilting her sideways, taking her
with him as he lay back on the bed. His hand
twined in her hair. He dragged her head back
from his shoulder and his mouth possessed hers
with rough hunger, his teeth bruising the tender
skin of her lips.

His savagery tasted sweet to Kirsty and
awakened a desire in her to rouse him further. No
longer shy, she caressed him, her hands touching
him wherever they could, her mouth feasting on
his.

'I love you, Kirsty,' he murmured against her
throat. 'I love you and I want you. Are you going
to marry me? Dare I ask you again?'

'Yes, I'm going to marry you,' she replied.
'Because I love and want you. I know now I want
to be a real wife and mother after all. I'm tired of
being subservient to an obsession.'

His lips sought hers again and again, and as the

weight of his hard sinewy thighs pressed against hers she knew she could no longer refuse the demands of his desire. Nor did she want to refuse. Her arms slid around him to hold him down against her, while her body twisted and lifted against his inviting invasion.

For a few moments she swung among stars and flew in outer space, then crying and sighing came slowly back to earth to the soft crushed firmness of the bed, to the silken hardness of his shoulder beneath her cheek and the warm velvet slackness of his limbs entwined with hers.

In the afterglow of fulfilment they slept a little, waking only when their limbs grew chilly. Neil pulled the quilt over them and within its shelter his lips worshipped her again. After a while she said,

'Shall we live at Balmore?'

'You can live there if you wish, but I won't be there all the time,' he answered, rubbing his nose against the soft curve of her cheek.

'Why?'

'My work as a surgeon still comes first and it always will. The reason I came back was not really because I wanted Balmore but was to take up a position at a teaching hospital in Edinburgh. I start there at the beginning of September.' His fingers played in her hair. 'Perhaps I should have told you this before I asked you to marry me, but do you think you can stand being left alone many times? Can you put up with a husband who's often late home? Or who has to leave suddenly in the middle of a dinner party to which you've invited important guests?' Bitterness rasped in his voice again and she guessed he was thinking of the way Barbara had behaved when he had been late or had left in the middle of dinner or even in the middle of the night.

'I'll be able to put up with having a surgeon for a husband because I love you,' she replied, tracing the line of his lips with the tip of her finger. 'I'll also have my own life to lead, you know, looking after our home and our children. And perhaps I'll have a job too, when the children are older, so you won't have to dance attendance on me all the time. We'll have a house near the hospital so you won't have far to go to work or to come home.'

'Sensible Kirsty,' he said. 'No wonder I love you.'

His lips claimed hers again and for a while there were no more words.

'But what about Balmore?' said Kirsty when, breathless from being overtaken by a new wave of passion, they lay relaxed in delicious lethargy.

'I've decided to give it to the National Trust, once I've inherited it,' he replied.

'All of it?'

'No. I've discussed the matter with Hamish and some of the other people who work on the estate. Archie Thornton and Will Andrews would both like to buy their farms, so I think we should give them the chance to buy at a low price in view of their long tenancies.' Neil rolled on to his back and stretched lazily. 'As for the rest, there's really too much of it to keep to ourselves, and I've never wanted to be an absentee landlord like my father was. I'd like to make it possible for more people to enjoy its beauty, so I've asked Doug Pettigrew to approach the Trust about offering it to them as a park. After the mortgage is paid off, of course.' He turned back to her and leaned up on an elbow. 'What do you think, Lady Whyte?' he asked.

'I think it's a wonderful idea. Will you give the house to the trust too?'

'No. We'll keep it with a few acres of land, for a place to retreat to and so that you can keep your hand in planting trees and gardening. I wouldn't like you to hanker too much after your job as factor,' he teased.

'Thank you,' she whispered, winding her arms about him and drawing him down. 'I think Alec would have approved.'

They kissed again, slowly and gently, enjoying their new freedom to caress each other without striving for culmination until both of them became aware of strange noises.

'It's me,' said Neil. 'I'm damned hungry—I haven't eaten since breakfast. Once I'd found out you were here I kept on coming.' He lifted his head and scowled down at her. 'You prevented me from having any dinner, so what are you going to do about it? Do you think they'll feed us here if we go and ask them nicely? Or should we drive into the nearest town and look for a fish and chip place?'

'They might feed us here. But where are you going to stay for the night? I know that every room has been booked in the hotel for the past few days.'

'I'm staying the night here,' he said, sliding off the bed and beginning to pull on his clothes. 'In the room next to this one. When I explained to the owner of the hotel that I'm a close ... very close friend of yours, she was most understanding and said she could let me have her daughter's room because the girl is away for the night. Not that I'll be needing a separate room, the way things have turned out,' he added, giving her a wicked glance over his shoulder. 'That bed is big enough for the two of us, as we've just proved.'

'Neil Dysart-Whyte, you are the most arrogant, conceited mischievous man I know!' Kirsty retorted, pausing in the middle of dressing herself to pick up a pillow and hurl it at him.

Laughing, Neil caught the pillow and hurled it back at her. She ducked, and the pillow hit the bedside lamp. The lamp slid to the edge of the bedside table wobbled, then fell to the floor with a crash. The light bulb shattered and the parchment shade became separated from its frame and crumpled.

'Oh, now look what you've done!' gasped Kirsty.

'You started it,' he replied, coming across to her and sliding his hands up her bare arms as if fascinated by their smooth silkiness. 'You started it four years ago when you came to the cottage on Cairn Rua. You're a dangerous lady,' he whispered, bending his head and tormenting the lobe of her ear.

'No, I'm not, I'm not! Please don't say that,' she protested, but she didn't pull away from him.

Her arms went round his neck and they stood close to each other. Her arms went round his neck and they stood close to each other, their bodies not quite touching, his hands at her waist. 'And I don't want to be dangerous,' she whispered. 'I just want to be loved.'

'And you shall be loved, my beloved temptress. You're tempting me to love you as you stand close to me with your shoulders gleaming white under the mantle of your black hair, your blue eyes dark and mysterious. A siren, that's what you are, tempting me to my downfall . . . and to go without my dinner.'

'But what are they going to think when we tell them about the broken lamp and when we don't go down again this evening to ask them for dinner?' asked Kirsty.

'*They* can think what they like, whoever *they* are. You and I are going to be much too busy making up for lost time, renewing our love for each other.' Neil's hands swept over her back as he pressed her against him. 'I told you it wasn't over, in the turret,' he whispered. 'I told you there were still some embers of love left just waiting to be fanned into a flame. Do you believe me now? Do you trust me now?' He pushed her away a little so that he could look into her eyes, the expression in his own one of doubt.

'Oh, yes, I trust you now,' she said sincerely, putting her arms around his neck again and lifting her face to his. 'You've rekindled the flame. I love you, I always have, but I wasn't sure about your feelings for me until today.'

The expression of doubt passed from his eyes like a cloud drifts away from the sun. Topaz-bright, his eyes glowed with passion before his lips possessed hers and she felt she was being kissed again by the young man she had met in the violet-tinted dusk of another summer evening. Her lost lover had come back to her at last, and as the flame of love burned steadily, fusing their hearts together, it was as if they had never been parted.

Harlequin® Plus
A WORD ABOUT THE AUTHOR

Ever since she can remember, Flora Kidd has cherished a longing to sail the seas—not on a big ocean liner, but in a sailboat. This great love brought her into contact with her husband-to-be, Wilf, who shared her dream. And over the years, they and their four children have sailed the waters of the Old World and the New (today they make their home in New Brunswick, one of Canada's Maritime provinces).

Flora's decision to write came about while she was living in a seaside village in the south of Scotland. Looking for something to read, she borrowed several romance novels and afterward remarked to a friend, "I think I could write a story like these." To which the friend replied, "Maybe you could, but would anyone want to read it?"

That was the necessary challenge! Flora's first Romance, *Nurse at Rowanbank* (#1058), was published in 1966 and her first Presents, *Dangerous Pretence* (#212), appeared in 1977. She is now a best-selling author of more than twenty Romances and fifteen Presents.

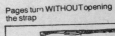
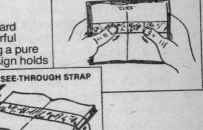